TIME

and three 10-minute plays

Philip Clay

Front cover image: AI image generated by Midjourney.

Inspiring Publishers
P.O. Box 159, Calwell, ACT Australia 2905
Email: publishaspg@gmail.com
http://www.inspiringpublishers.com

A catalogue record for this book is available from the National Library of Australia

National Library of Australia The Prepublication Data Service

Author: Philip Clay
Title: Time and three 10-minute plays
Genre: Fiction

Paperback ISBN: 978-1-923250-41-3
ePub2 ISBN: 978-1-923250-42-0

Table of Contents

About the Writer

Philip Clay has been a lawyer for most of his working life. First as a solicitor then barrister and appointed Senior Counsel in 2011. Philip's last job as a lawyer prior to retirement due to ill health was an Acting Commissioner of the Land and Environment Court of New South Wales from 2019 – 2021.

After retirement Philip took the opportunity to return to his love of writing and also become involved with Manly Theatre Group (MTG), a community based theatre group on Sydney's northern beaches which began in 2022. Philip has been with MTG since its inception and has been a committee member, Vice President and also served as President.

Until MTG, Philip's writing outside the law has been limited to melodramas performed for aged persons homes and revues performed at schools his children have attended. Philip's flair as a trivia night host is remembered by many.

Apart from "performing" in real life as a barrister, Philip has performed on stage in revues and more recently in plays presented by Pymble Players on Sydney's north shore.

About the Plays

TIME premiered at the Darley Smith Theatre in Manly on 27 July 2023. It was presented by Manly Theatre Group.

It was directed by Stan Kouros and produced by Philip Clay.

BUS STOP was a finalist in the Peoples' Choice Section of the Short+Sweet Festival Sydney 2022. It was also short listed for a number of other Short+Sweet Festivals internationally. Translated into Tamil it was a Peoples' Choice finalist in Short+Sweet South India.

BUS STOP was performed as a radio play by Script in Hand in 2022. BUS STOP was also presented at the Manly Theatre Group Festival of Short Plays in 2022.

MANHOOD was a Peoples' Choice semi-finalist in the Short+Sweet Festival Hollywood in 2024. It was also performed at the Manly Festival of Short Plays in 2023.

FANTASY was performed at the Manly Festival of Short Plays in 2023.

Acknowledgments

My Manly Theatre Group "family" have been hugely supportive in this endeavour and special thanks to Zoe Hudson, Angharad Thompson Rees, Mauricio Espinoza and Anna Rezenbrink for their guidance and, always positive, criticism.

I am indebted to the lessons learnt at Gotham Writers and especially Richard Caliban for his incisive and direct guidance in the development of the script for TIME.

And thank you so much to Robyn and my family. No need to say anymore.

TIME

For dad

CAST

BESSIE, 75 years old with later stage dementia.

MARTHA, Bessie's elder child (of 2), age 50s. Twice divorced, self-centred

CHARLIE, Bessie's son and younger child, age 40s, subsistence farmer

JENNY, Charlie's former partner/girlfriend, sensible, age 30s/40s

PENNY, Charlie's current girlfriend, "skank", bubbly, mischievous age 30s

GEORGE, Bessie's 70 year old younger brother, largely deaf, father of Ross

ROSS, George's son, 30s/40s, successful lawyer

ZOLA, a nurse at Bessie's nursing home

SCENE 1

The present

SCENE: BESSIE'S nursing home room.

(BESSIE sits on a chair apparently looking out the window. She does not move but continues the gaze. A nurse is in the room tidying up. Bessie and the nurse could be on stage when the audience is coming in.)

ZOLA: Big day today Bessie.

(Bessie does not move or respond)
(Moving to Bessie to look at her)
            Let me look at you – ready for your party

(Bessie does not move or respond)
(Zola looks out the window too.)

            It's a lovely day for a birthday picnic. All the family will be there I'm sure. You just sit tight while I tidy up in here. *(Pause)* Charlie will be along shortly to get you. Oh no, hang on, your daughter is coming he said. I haven't met her before. Not sure she's ever been here. I can't remember what Charlie said her name is. Anyway, shouldn't be too long now.

(Zola freezes in action while the Bessie speech happens)

BESSIE: The words don't seem to come out anymore. At least I don't think they do. They're in my head. But they don't always make sense. It's just a jumbled mess....

Party. Picnic. I wondered why they dressed me up like this. 75. Yes I'm 75. Today I turn 75.

You wouldn't know would you? Sometimes ... or nearly always I wouldn't know.

Most of the time I don't know who I am. Or where I am. Or why. I don't even know Charlie when he comes to see me.

But then, I don't know that I don't know. When I don't know. If you know what I mean.

Sometimes though, I know. And I know that I know. Then I think I know Charlie. I know he talks to me and tells me things. And then I know those things.

(*Shouts or shrieks*)
Oh no. Don't. Stop.

(*Bessie takes a little longer to recover without knowing what really happened.*)

It's like a light has come on. And another. And another. And more. My mind awakes as if to a vibrant dawn. It's so bright I can see today and yesterday and all the days of my life. Flashing before my very eyes. I am alive.

But then, after a minute, or a few minutes, some time. The lights begin to go out. One by one. I desperately reach for the switch to stop them going off. I don't want to lose the light again. But I can't find the switch. And I realise there is no switch. There's nothing. Nothing I can do.

The darkness in my mind returns and I don't know anymore. Without knowing that I don't know. I've forgotten, without knowing I ever knew.

Today, now, I can't talk, but I know. I know there's a picnic lunch for my birthday. With Martha, and …. and ….. Oh, I don't know.

(*Bessie retreats*)

ZOLA: Shouldn't be long now Bessie. Have a lovely day.

(*Zola exits*)

(*Bessie does not move or respond.*)

END SCENE 1

SCENE 2

Some weeks earlier

SCENE: *There is a caravan backdrop with a door (there can be alternate ways of putting the "caravan" on stage). There are some scattered chairs and a table outside.*

(*CHARLIE enters carrying a chainsaw.*)

CHARLIE: (*calling out*) I'm back Penny.

PENNY: (*From inside caravan*) Hi, I'm in here.

CHARLIE: Another one bites the dust. (*Puts chainsaw down*)

(*PENNY enters coming out caravan door, drinking a beer and carrying another can of beer.*)

PENNY: Success?

CHARLIE: Yep, it never had a fucking chance. A biggie too.

PENNY: How much will you get for it?

CHARLIE: Could be 70 - 80 bucks I reckon.

PENNY: That'd be good. Keep us in beer for a while.

CHARLIE: Yeah, anyway, we'll see when Stan drops by.

PENNY: Who's Stan?

CHARLIE: Timber yard guy. Does firewood too.

(*Charlie sits down*)

PENNY: Beer?

CHARLIE: Come here my lovely.

(*PENNY thinks he's referring to her but CHARLIE takes the beer*)

CHARLIE: Ta (*CHARLIE takes a sip*) Aaaah

(*They sit quietly to enjoy the quiet.*)

(*CHARLIE'S mobile phone rings*)

CHARLIE: Hello
             Hello Martha ….. no not at all, always got time for you Martha. Not that that's much of my time……. nothing, just .. no, nothing. What do you want Martha?
             I know. Next month.
             I know that too.
             What do you want Martha?
             I see.
             Here?
             Yes Martha.
             Yes Martha.
             Of course, if that's what you want Martha.
             I get it Martha.
             Leave the nursing home to me and I'll ring Uncle George as well.
             Yes you do that. If there is anyone else.
             Yes Martha.
             Bye Martha.

PENNY: Who was that?

CHARLIE: (*Looks at Penny as if to say "isn't it obvious"*) Martha.

PENNY: Your sister Martha?

CHARLIE: Is there any other?

PENNY: What does she want you to do now?

CHARLIE: To help her organize a birthday party for Mum's 75th.

PENNY: Oh that's nice of her, for once.

CHARLIE: Sure, except what she really means is that I'm supposed to do everything and she'll come down from her commune for the birthday lunch.

PENNY: Oh shit, so typical. She expects you to do everything. Still. So where is it happening, this party she's "organizing"?

CHARLIE: Here.

PENNY: Here? You mean, here? Surely you didn't offer to have it here? In the van?

CHARLIE: No she just said, "you can have it there".

PENNY: And you didn't say no.

CHARLIE: I couldn't.

PENNY: You could have.

CHARLIE: Well I didn't.

PENNY: Is she going to pay for the food and stuff?

CHARLIE: She didn't say.

PENNY: You didn't ask her did you?

CHARLIE: I didn't. I couldn't.

PENNY: You could have Charlie. Charlie, Charlie, Charlie.

CHARLIE: She's family.

PENNY: All the more reason she should be doing something and not just telling you to do it.

CHARLIE: I'll talk to her at the lunch. But you know there's no point arguing with Martha. She gets her way, always has.

PENNY: It's just not fair Charlie. On you. Or on me for that matter. If I count.

CHARLIE: Of course you count. (*Shrugs*) What am I supposed to do?

PENNY: Tell that bitch it's not good enough. That's what.

CHARLIE: Yeah, that'll really work.

PENNY: How are we going to pay for this if Martha puts in exactly nuthin'?

CHARLIE: I'll just have to knock out more trees. I'll see how many more Stan can take. I reckon we'll get enough money that way. We're not going to give 'em fillet steak you know.

(*Pause*)

PENNY: Are you going to the nursing home this afternoon?

CHARLIE: I should. I haven't been this week yet.

PENNY: Your mother won't know that.

CHARLIE: Maybe not. But still, I reckon I should go today.

PENNY: Got to keep in her good books.

CHARLIE: Yeah, her good books. But you know, like I reckon some of the nurses keep their own "good books". They watch out how many times you've been and stuff I reckon. So bloody judgy.

PENNY: Hey, maybe they're running a sweep – or betting on how many visitors all those "out of it" people are getting. You should ask for a share of the money if Bessie is the winner. But I reckon it's Bessie's good books that are the important ones.

CHARLIE: (*Grunts*) Sure. You stayin' here tonight?

PENNY: Of course Charlie boy, where else would I wanna be? But you'd better have a shower after you've been chopping down them trees.

CHARLIE: Deal.

PENNY: And I reckon we oughta work out what you can do about bloody Martha.

CHARLIE: That's what Jenny tried and look what happened.

PENNY: Bugger Jenny.

CHARLIE: No comment. I'll shower and go and see Mum. Won't be too long, you'll be ok?

PENNY: So long as there's beer, I'll be fine.

CHARLIE: That's my girl.

(*CHARLIE exits into caravan.*)

(*PENNY sits and drinks her beer. Empties can and goes inside to get another from fridge in Caravan and returns.*)

(*JENNY enters*)

JENNY: (*Calls out as she enters*) Hello.

PENNY: Well look what the cat dragged in. Didn't expect to see you here.

JENNY: Who did you expect? Your parole officer?

PENNY: (*Looking back at door*) Shut the fuck up will ya. What do ya want anyway?

JENNY: I want to speak to Charlie.

PENNY: Well you can't.

JENNY: Why not?

PENNY: He's in the shower.

JENNY: I assume he'll get out eventually. I'll wait.

PENNY: What do you want him for?

JENNY: That's between him and me. Nothing to do with you.

PENNY: Charlie is everything to do with me. Tell me. Or get out of here.

JENNY: It's just between him and me.

PENNY: Nothing's just between you and him, not since you dumped him.

(PENNY *approaches JENNY in a menacing manner. JENNY begins to back away.*)

JENNY: (*Nervously*) Don't you touch me.

PENNY: I think it's time you left. NOW.

JENNY: (*Begins to leave*) Tell him to return my calls. It's important. I can't wait much longer… before it gets serious. I really don't want to have to call in the lawyers.

PENNY: What do ya mean, lawyers?

JENNY   Charlie knows.

PENNY: Well I wanna know.

JENNY: You ask him. And tell him to talk to me.

(JENNY *exits.* PENNY *sits with her beer. Contemplates. Then calls out.*)

PENNY: Charlie, we need to talk.

(CHARLIE *enters from caravan. Wet hair etc*)

CHARLIE: What did ya say?

PENNY: Your ex was just here.

CHARLIE: What did she want?

PENNY: She said you had to call her or she's getting a lawyer on the job.

CHARLIE: Shit.

PENNY: What's goin' on Charlie? Why would she need to get a bloody lawyer?

CHARLIE: Don't worry. I'll sort it out.

PENNY: What is it Charlie?

CHARLIE: She reckons I owe her some money. I'll talk to her and sort it out.

PENNY: Money? How much money?

CHARLIE: It doesn't matter. I'll sort it. I'd better go.

(CHARLIE *exits*)

PENNY: (*calls*) But you've got no money Charlie. (*To herself*) At least not until … your mother ….

END SCENE 2

SCENE 3

Later the same day

The scene is Bessie's nursing home room. She is sitting in a chair gazing out the window.

CHARLIE and ZOLA enter and pause at the doorway.

CHARLIE: How is she today Zola?

ZOLA: Much the same as usual, I guess. There are moments, you know, when she is a bit brighter. But they don't seem to last that long.

CHARLIE: She's always just looking out the window.

ZOLA: That's what she does most of the time when she's in her room. We take her to the common room as much as we can for a change of scenery. She seems happy enough. Who knows what goes on in her mind these days? Always a mystery. I'll leave you to it.

CHARLIE: Thanks Zola. Hi Mum.

          (No response from BESSIE. CHARLIE moves closer and gets in Bessie's eye line.)

          Hi Mum.

BESSIE: Oh. Hello (*No recognition*)

CHARLIE: It's me, Charlie.

BESSIE: Hello Charlie (*without warmth, as if to a stranger*)

CHARLIE: Your son. Charlie, your boy.

BESSIE: My boy Charlie (*still not recognising, then a glimmer*). Aren't you growing up? Let me look at you. So tall, like your Dad. How was school today?

CHARLIE: I'm not at school anymore Mum.

BESSIE: Why not? Did he... are you hurt... ? Did they send you home?

CHARLIE: I'm 42 Mum. And Dad's ....

BESSIE: You haven't been expelled have you?

CHARLIE: No Mum. No, school was great. It's over for the day, that's all. How are you?

BESSIE does not respond and returns to gazing out the window. CHARLIE sits with resignation.

CHARLIE: What's the point? I wish I knew. I'm here, I'm not here, I'm a kid, I'm an adult. Or .... I'm nothing. Actually, now it's nothing most of the time. Why do I bother? Because I'd feel guilty if I didn't. Martha would make sure I felt guilty. (*Mimicking*) "Oh Charlie, I live hours away and you're just there. I'll come when I can but you've got to look after her Charlie" in that fake accent of hers. It's been the same fucking story forever.

(*CHARLIE now turns to talk to his mother*)

I'm sorry Mum, it's not your fault, not anymore.

Anyway, it's your birthday in a few weeks. You're gunna be 75 and we'll have a birthday picnic lunch for you. Get you out of here for a few hours. Martha is coming down, well today she says she'll be coming down, and I'll see if Uncle George can come up from Sydney. And I'll ask anyone else I can think of. We'll make a big party of it.

Ok Mum? Something to look forward to. (*Still no response from Bessie.*) I may as well go. Bye Mum. See you soon.

(*CHARLIE goes and bends to kiss her on the cheek. BESSIE has no immediate reaction. CHARLIE pauses then stands and turns to leave. BESSIE turns her head to look at CHARLIE as he leaves.*)

BESSIE: Good bye …… Ernie.

CHARLIE drops his shoulders in disappointment.

Zola appears at doorway

ZOLA: Everything okay Charlie?

CHARLIE: Yeah, it's fine.

ZOLA: It's just I was next door and I heard you talking.

CHARLIE: Oh sorry Zola, I didn't mean to be loud.

ZOLA: Not a problem at all at my end Charlie. Just wanted to make sure everything is okay.

CHARLIE: Yeah. 15th of next month it's her birthday, she'll be 75. We're having a family party or picnic, so we'll take her out for the day.

ZOLA: That will be lovely. She'll enjoy that.

CHARLIE: Will she Zola? Will she really? I just don't know anymore. Is it worth the bother taking her anywhere, or even coming to see her? I wish I knew. Then at least I'd know it's worthwhile, all the time I spend coming, instead of ….

[*Unsaid – getting on with my life*]

ZOLA: I wish I knew too Charlie. What she thinks, whether she does think, how she feels, or what she feels. But we can never know for sure. People like your Mum are still human beings Charlie, and that's why we encourage family to visit as much as possible, because it just might make a difference to their lives.

And we can't say it won't make a difference, Charlie. We can never say that. It's just a little happiness even if it is just a moment. And then we feel it, you'd feel it too Charlie, that you've done something good.

CHARLIE: Yeah. Well. I guess. I dunno. I just dunno. But thanks for that. (*Sighs*) Anyway this little ray of sunshine has got to go. See you next time.

END SCENE 3

SCENE 4

Evening, the same day or within a few days.

SCENE   GEORGE'S *lounge room featuring simply a
                chair, a side table and a TV. GEORGE is seated
                in the lounge chair watching TV. The volume is
                very loud*

                *A mobile phone rings. GEORGE doesn't notice
                it. It rings out.*

                *Phone rings again and GEORGE realizes after a
                couple of rings. He then stands looks around for
                it , can't find it in time and it rings out.*

                *Phone rings again. GEORGE keeps looking and
                finds it in his pocket. Answers.*

GEORGE: Hello.

(Light comes up on CHARLIE on the phone.)

CHARLIE: Uncle George

GEORGE: Hello

CHARLIE: *(Talking loudly, practically shouting)* Uncle
                George, it's Charlie.

GEORGE: Hello, who is this?

CHARLIE: Can you turn down the TV?

GEORGE: Hang on, I'll turn down the TV.

(GEORGE *turns down the TV.*)

Hello.

CHARLIE: Hi Uncle George, it's Charlie.

GEORGE: Who?

CHARLIE: Charlie.

GEORGE: Oh, I was hoping it was Ross.

CHARLIE: Sorry, but it's me.

GEORGE: Didn't mean it like that Charlie, sorry. It's just that he said he'd ring me today.

CHARLIE: And obviously he hasn't yet.

GEORGE: No. Anyway. What can I do for you Charlie boy, this is an unexpected pleasure.

CHARLIE: Mum's turning 75 in a few weeks and I was wondering if you could come up here for a picnic lunch to celebrate.

GEORGE: Of course, I'd love to come up for my big sister's birthday. But I'll have to check with Ross, cause he'd have to come too, it's too far for me to drive. Will that be okay?

CHARLIE: Yeah, no worries.

GEORGE: He always seems so busy, I hope he can do it. What's the date?

CHARLIE: We're planning for the 15th, here at the farm, so pretty casual. You check with Ross and I'll text you the address and the best way to get here.

GEORGE: Goodo. I'll let you know, usual time when we talk next week. But hopefully it'll be fine. How's things otherwise?

CHARLIE: Can't complain…. no point really.

GEORGE: Yeah me too. No one'll listen. (*Chuckles*)

CHARLIE: Anyway, I've got to go and chop down some trees. Talk next week. Oh and don't forget to take your tablets.

GEORGE: Yeah, yeah, okay Charlie. Bye.

(*They both hang up. Light goes off CHARLIE but stays on GEORGE.*)

(*GEORGE looks at his watch. Then at the phone. Thinks about ringing [ROSS] and almost does so, then feels some stomach pain and tosses the phone onto the side table. He then takes a couple of tablets(painkillers) from a packet and downs them with some water. George sits and turns up the TV. He then looks at his watch again…*).

GEORGE: Bugger it. I'll ring him.

(*GEORGE dials number and waits for answer.*)

GEORGE: Bugger. (*Leaves message*) Ross, it's Dad. Give me a call eh? Soon as you can.

(*GEORGE manages to fall asleep. Lights dim. He then awakes with a start.*)

GEORGE: Bugger. I've missed the end of Vera. Who did it?

(GEORGE *looks at phone and sees there's been no message from Ross and he hasn't rung.*)

GEORGE: Text. I'll send a text.

(GEORGE *types out a message on the phone with a big smile. Puts down the phone and resumes watching TV. He turns it down a bit. Leans back in the chair and his eyes close. Light dims to signal the passing of time.*)

(*Sound of key in door and door opens as lights come up. GEORGE remains apparently asleep for the moment. ROSS enters.*)

ROSS: Oh my god Dad are you .....

GEORGE: (*Wakes*) Hello son.

ROSS: Dad, thank God. I thought you were ...

GEORGE: What? Dead?

ROSS: Yeah, well. Are you okay?

GEORGE: I'm fine.

ROSS: Really?

GEORGE: Yep.

ROSS: What about the heart attack?

GEORGE: What heart attack?

ROSS: The one in the message you sent me.

GEORGE: Message?

ROSS: The text message. (ROSS *pulls out his phone.*) The one that said "I think I'm having a heart attack. Plea ..." You didn't even finish the message.

GEORGE: Oh that message.

ROSS: Yes that message.

GEORGE: Well it seems it wasn't a heart attack after all.

ROSS: Should I take you to the hospital anyway? Did you have chest pains?

GEORGE: I thought they might be coming.

ROSS: What? Pre chest pain chest pains?

GEORGE: Something like that. Without the pain. Just a feeling that chest pain was on the way.

ROSS: Jesus Christ, I'm here on false pretences, aren't I? I got this message, it seemed like you were dying, and I came straight away, pretty much.

GEORGE: Now that you're here ....

ROSS: Now that I'm here? Now that I'm here? I have to go. Bad joke Dad. I've got people at home I'll need to explain this to. Why I had to leave for a false alarm. Embarrassing Dad.

GEORGE: Oh just listen for a minute will you? Charlie rang me.

ROSS: Who's Charlie?

GEORGE: Your cousin Charlie.

ROSS: Oh, what did he want? (*Disinterested*)

GEORGE: There's a birthday party for Bessie next month, 15th. She'll be 75. I want to go of course but I'll need you to take me. It's too far for me to drive by myself.

ROSS: I thought Bessie was in a home and pretty much out of it.

GEORGE: Whatever, there's going to be a party and I need you to take me.

ROSS: Let me check. (*Looks at calendar on phone*) Yeah, well, okay, that's fine. It'll be a whole bloody day I suppose.

GEORGE: And there's something else.

ROSS: Can it wait? I'll call you. Or we can talk at your next "not a heart attack" moment?

GEORGE: Well …

ROSS: I really don't have much time.

GEORGE: Okay, yeah, you go. Next time.

ROSS: Next time. See ya Dad. (ROSS *rushes off stage*)

GEORGE: See ya son.

END SCENE 4

SCENE 5

A few weeks later. Today.

SCENE: CHARLIE'S CARAVAN

There are two picnic chairs side by side in front of the caravan. A picnic table (big enough to seat 6) with various foods and a bottle of red wine, plastic glasses and paper plates is to the side. An esky is beside the picnic table. A few other picnic chairs are scattered around.

The scene opens with an empty stage. CHARLIE enters from the caravan carrying a few glasses which he puts on the table. He then gets a bottle of beer from the esky opens it, sits, and has a drink. He looks at his watch. He stretches out on the chair to relax. A moment later he hears the noise off stage of a car pulling up and parking. He looks in that direction, puts the bottle of beer on the table and begins to walk in that direction as ROSS enters.

PENNY is not there at the moment.

CHARLIE: Ross!

ROSS: Charlie, good to see you.

(They hesitatingly go for the embrace and end up shaking hands.)

CHARLIE: Been a while.

ROSS: Yeah, guess I haven't seen you since Mum's funeral.

CHARLIE: Yeaaaah. Naaah. Wasn't there actually. Couldn't make it.

ROSS: Right.

CHARLIE: Hey, want a beer? (*He goes to esky*) Where's Uncle George? He told me you were coming with him. He was very pleased he didn't have to drive all this way by himself.

(*Hands beer*)

ROSS: Thanks. (*Looks at beer.*) Don't know this one. 5X?

CHARLIE: Yeah just like 4X but 25% better, so they say.

ROSS: Riiight. Where do you get it?

CHARLIE: Aldi.

ROSS: That explains it. Good. Different.

CHARLIE: You were going to tell me where George is.

ROSS: Yeah, sorry. Anyway, I dropped him off at the nursing home so he could have a chat to your Mum there first, just the two of them. Martha can bring him down when she picks up your Mum. (*hesitates*) Um, Dad told you I was coming with him? (*puzzled*)

CHARLIE: Yep

ROSS: Aha.

CHARLIE: Yeah, a few weeks ago when I first told him about Mum's party he said he'd ask you but wasn't sure if you would. You know whether you'd have the time to come up. Fair way from Sydney.

ROSS: Well, not really that far. But I don't get it. You've spoken to him recently? He didn't tell me.

CHARLIE: Yeah well, he rings each week.

ROSS: Jesus, each week. Must be a bit of a pain for you.

CHARLIE: Not really, happy to chat. I got the time.

ROSS: Yeah well, Dad and I are always talking. He must have just forgot to mention it. (*Beat*) So how's Aunty Bessie?

CHARLIE: Ohhh much the same the last year or two. I go and see her every few days, but I don't think she knows who I am anymore, most of the time. Or all of the time, I can't tell. She seems to come good every now and again, for a bit. So the nurses tell me. I haven't seen it too much lately.

ROSS: That's hard. I mean for you.

CHARLIE: Yeah...probably worse for her. Sometimes she talks about things from ages ago and even there was once she thought I was Dad. That was weird.

ROSSs: Yeah.

CHARLIE: Dad's been dead over 20, 30 years ..... and she can still think he's there.

ROSS: The mind plays funny tricks sometimes.

CHARLIE: She smiles, or she nods sometimes, but she seems pretty much out of it most of the time.

ROSS: Physically ok?

CHARLIE: Yeah, they say she's fit as a mallee bull. If a mallee bull was 75 years old …. But there's no particular health problems I don't think.

ROSS: Well that's something, I suppose.

CHARLIE: I guess. Not sure what though. Not doing her any good in the nursing home. She's not exactly running laps of the garden and they can't let her out by herself anyway.

(Pause for a few beats as they search for something to say, each takes a drink of beer.)

ROSS: So this is the legendary farm eh? Didn't see your farmhouse on the way in. Should give us a tour later.

CHARLIE: Yep, not much to see though. Really you're looking at it now.

ROSS: Right. I see. Nursing home in town is not that far. That's good.

CHARLIE: Yeah, nah, not far at all.

ROSS: Easy to go in to see Aunty Bessie.

(Pause for a couple of beats. Looks with feigned admiration at the caravan)

Good to have the van as well.

CHARLIE: Yeah.

ROSS: Can get away a bit I suppose.

CHARLIE: Could do.

ROSS: Cool. Use it much?

CHARLIE: Yep. (*beat*) Every day.

ROSS: Really?

CHARLIE: Yep, I live in it. It's home. My "homestead" (*ironically*).

ROSS: Sorry, so there's no farmhouse here.

CHARLIE: Nah, this is it.

ROSS: Looks ... good.

CHARLIE: Does the job.

ROSS: What a lifestyle eh? The freedom. Go where you want, do what you like, always your "homestead" with you… (*laughs*)

CHARLIE: (*Ironically/bitterly*) Yeah, livin' the dream. In a van on a scrappy block of land in the middle of nowhere, goin' to the nursing home every few days just to make sure my mother's not dead…. yet. Yep, freedom. You can't beat it.

(*Pause for a few beats as they search for something to say, each takes a drink of beer.*)

ROSS: Not working though?

CHARLIE: Nothing much. I cut down timber on the farm and sell it to a local timber yard – they use it for timber or firewood. And pay me cash.

ROSS: You got that much dead timber you can take out?

CHARLIE: It's not all dead timber. I just got a lot of trees. Look around.

ROSS: And it's ok to cut them down? Don't need a permit or something?

CHARLIE: My farm. My trees. No one knows, too far out of the way.

ROSS: Yeeaahh, but the environment, you know, biodiversity and all that, you usually need a permit, I think, to cut down trees, even in the bush.

CHARLIE: Like I said. My farm, my trees. I mean if I chop down a tree in a forest and no-one sees, did it really happen? (*Chuckles*)

(*Pause for a few beats*)

CHARLIE: Any trees on your place?

ROSS: Well, not really.

CHARLIE: They'd block the harbour view eh?

ROSS: Yeah, well, maybe. I haven't chopped any down at least. Pretty conscious of doing the right thing.

CHARLIE: The right thing in the city's a bit different to out here. Pretty easy for you not to chop down any trees. Big city lawyers usually don't have to sell firewood to get by. (*Laughs*)

ROSS: But we all have a responsibility don't we, to our children and their children to look after the environment?

CHARLIE: Well, I don't have any children.

ROSS: Still that's why you're supposed to get a permit. To make sure it's ok for the environment to chop down the trees.

CHARLIE: Yeah... huh... I see your.... your point. I guess maybe it's uh... its not the—the same out here like in the — where you are. But I mean yeah — choppin' down trees is... is... maybe ... shouldn't.. whatever

(*Pause for a few beats*)

ROSS: And I've forgotten your partner's name ... sorry ... (*Struggles to remember Jenny's name*)

CHARLIE: You're probably thinking of Jenny... but ...

(*Noise of car off stage*)

Ah, here they are.

(*Martha rushes on to the stage*)

ROSS: Martha! (*Trying to get Martha's attention*) Hi Martha

MARTHA: (*Ignoring Ross talking to Charlie*) You won't believe what happened.

CHARLIE: What?

ROSS: Where are the others?

MARTHA: Hi Ross. I've left them at the nursing home. I said I'll go back in 10 minutes after I drop off some stuff here.

CHARLIE: What's up?

MARTHA: Well I'm there at the nursing home and they're talking, well Uncle George is talking. Mum as usual is not saying anything. Incidentally, I didn't know he was going to the nursing home. You should have told me Charlie. Anyway, George says to Mum, and I quote : "Such a pity that Charlie and Jenny have split up. They were together for such a long time."

CHARLIE: So what?

MARTHA: Charlie, can't you see?

ROSS: (*To* CHARLIE) You and Jenny have split up?

MARTHA: They have, but we haven't told Mum. I don't want her to be told stuff that might upset her - Charlie knows that.

ROSS: Oh. Sorry, Charlie, I didn't know.

CHARLIE: I told Uncle George ages ago, I didn't tell him not to say anything to Mum.

ROSS: Well he didn't say anything to me. Sorry he spilled the beans to Bessie.

MARTHA: Oh it's not your Dad's fault. He didn't know she didn't know.

ROSS: I didn't know I didn't know.

CHARLIE: Did she say anything?

MARTHA: No, I'm not sure it sunk in. Actually I'm not sure it even got to the surface let alone sinking in.

CHARLIE: She'll soon forget anyway. Don't worry about it. It doesn't matter.

MARTHA: Yes you're probably right. She won't remember even if she heard.

ROSS: Why is it a secret anyway? Shouldn't she know?

CHARLIE: Ask Martha, It was her dumb idea.

MARTHA: Well, before she became … well, before she had to go into the nursing home, everything in her eyes was perfect. We both had partners, who she liked, or loved, a lot. We didn't want to take away that memory for her. Well, I didn't, Charlie may have thought differently, but we haven't told her.

ROSS: You don't think she has the right to know? I assume she's not totally out of it all the time.

CHARLIE: That's what I thought.

MARTHA: Why spoil a good story with the truth? Anyway, it is what it is, she doesn't know, and I have no intention of telling her. Right Charlie?

CHARLIE: Yes Martha. Jenny says she's coming you know.

MARTHA: Fine. You can tell her not to say you've split up.

CHARLIE: Suuuure. Penny will be here too.

ROSS: Who's Penny?

MARTHA: The "new" Jenny.

CHARLIE: My new girlfriend.

ROSS: (*Confused*) There's a Penny and a Jenny and they're both going to be here, but you don't want your mother to know that you and Jenny have split up?

CHARLIE: They both want to be here. Jenny to wish Mum happy birthday and Penny just to meet Mum for the first time. I couldn't say no to either of them.

ROSS: (*Jokingly*) Are they doing shifts? Have you given them time slots?

CHARLIE: Not exactly. (*Pause for a beat*) Penny doesn't know Jenny will be here. They sorta don't get along.

MARTHA: (*Sighs*) Look, don't worry, maybe Mum won't know the difference, she'll just be happy to see people. She won't know who is who, or what's what. I'm sure we can pull it off, and I really don't want her upset. I'll think of something.

ROSS: I'll tell Dad not to talk about it again, at least not to Aunty Bessie.

MARTHA: Actually, with Jenny coming I don't suppose Penny could just disappear for a while?

CHARLIE: No, I can't just make her disappear Martha. Jesus.

MARTHA: And where is Penny anyway?

CHARLIE: She's gone to town to get some ice and a few other things I forgot.

MARTHA: Classic Charlie. Can't even get a basic lunch organised on time. How long will she be?

CHARLIE: Oh, not long. She'll be here when you get back.

MARTHA: (*To Ross*) Oh and we haven't said a proper hello. Helloooo

ROSS: (*at the same time*) Hellooo

(*They embrace, without hesitation*)

MARTHA: Look, I'd better go back and get them. I just wanted to let you know what I heard. See you in about ten minutes. Charlie please get everything ready eh? (*Starts to leave*) Oh, and Ross, the other thing we haven't told Mum - I've divorced Colin. Bye, see you soon.

(*Martha swiftly walks off stage*)

ROSS: What did she say? She and Colin are divorced?

CHARLIE: Yep

ROSS: That's her second divorce isn't it?

CHARLIE: Oh yeah, she does divorce very well that sister of mine.

ROSS: And she hasn't told your mother? Her mother?

CHARLIE: Nup

ROSS: Riiiight. And is Colin coming too?

CHARLIE: Not sure, I left that with Martha. Be interesting
             if he does.

ROSS: Yep. Sounds like it will be interesting anyway.
             (*beat*) So … Dad knew you'd split with Jenny.

CHARLIE: Yep.

ROSS: Wish he'd bloody told me.

CHARLIE: Look, I'll get the salads and the other stuff ready.
             As much as I can before Penny gets back.

(*CHARLIE enters the van leaving ROSS alone on stage. He sits
on a chair, drinks some beer. Maybe looks at it disparagingly.*)

ROSS: (*To himself*) Not exactly Peroni. Aldi crap. Shit,
             what a great way to spend a Sunday.

(PENNY *enters with the shopping and puts it on the table*)

PENNY: Well, hello. I bet you're Ross.

ROSS: Yes. I am indeed Ross. And I bet you're Penny.

PENNY: Got it in one, sunshine.

(PENNY *puts the ice in the esky, flops on the chair and pulls a
beer from the esky.*)

PENNY: Geez, been so hangin' for this. Cheers. Where's
             Charlie?

ROSS: Inside getting stuff ready.

PENNY: Good boy.

ROSS: So, you living here too?

PENNY: Yeah, pretty much. Charlie and I get on good and the rent's cheap – know what I mean?

ROSS: I think … yeah, sure … I think …

PENNY: Hang on, Jesus, don't tell Charlie I said it that way. He's my boyfriend and all, but, you know, who knows.

ROSS: My lips are sealed.

PENNY: I bloody hope so.

ROSS: Should be a nice little party today. I guess the others will be here soon.

PENNY: Yeah, the old dear is 75. According to Charlie she's pretty much out of it so I'm not exactly sure why bloody Martha demanded a party. Waste of money I reckon.

ROSS: Well, we're here now.

PENNY: Yeah we're here alright. And she's there in the nursing home, still carrying on. You'd think Bessie would do the right thing and ….

(*Enter* CHARLIE *from caravan.*)

PENNY: Hi honey, I've met your cutey pie cousin here.

CHARLIE: That's nice. Where's the shopping?

PENNY: Over there.

CHARLIE: Um, wanna give us a hand Penny?

PENNY: Sure, hun.

(CHARLIE *and* PENNY *enter caravan*)

ROSS: Jesus. It's not getting any better. (*shakes head drinks beer.*)

END SCENE 5

SCENE 6

SCENE: CHARLIE'S farm outside the caravan, as before.

(*Lights come up on stage. ROSS is still the only one there.*)

(*Noise of car off stage*)

ROSS:　　　(*Calls out*) I reckon that's the others Charlie, they're here.

(*CHARLIE comes out of the caravan*)

CHARLIE:　　Well, here we go. Can you finish off please Penny?

(*Enter MARTHA followed by BESSIE and GEORGE*)

MARTHA:　　Hello, we're all here.

ROSS:　　　Hello Aunty Bessie (*as he approaches her*).

(*Bessie gives Ross a blank look as he bends to give her a kiss on the cheek.*)

It's me Ross, your nephew. George's son.

(*Bessie gives an "almost" smile but does not speak*)

MARTHA:　　Mum you come over here and sit, and George can sit next to you.

(Martha steers Bessie to one of the two chairs in front of the caravan.)

GEORGE: Charlie ….

(George heads over to talk to Charlie but is intercepted by Ross)

ROSS: Dad, Dad.

GEORGE: (*Irritably*) I'm just saying hello to Charlie.

ROSS: Hang on just a sec.

GEORGE: (*Not hearing properly*) What?

ROSS: Hang on a sec, I need to tell you something.

GEORGE: (*Not hearing properly*) What?

ROSS: (*In a low voice*) Bessie doesn't know that Charlie and Jenny have split up.

GEORGE: (*Not hearing*) Eh?

ROSS: (*Still in a low voice*) Bessie doesn't know that Charlie and Jenny have split up.

GEORGE: (*Loudly*) Speak up I can hardly hear you.

ROSS: (*Louder*) Bessie doesn't know that Charlie and Jenny have split up.

GEORGE: Yes she does.

ROSS: No she doesn't.

GEORGE: Yes she does…. I told her.

ROSS: Well, no one else has and they want to keep it that way. So maybe don't mention it again. And you never told me…

GEORGE: (*Interrupts*)

Charlie, come and say g'day to your old uncle.

(Charlie and George move towards each other. They shake hands warmly.)

CHARLIE: G'day Uncle George.

GEORGE: Nice to see you Charlie. Thanks for putting this on.

CHARLIE: Glad you could make it. How are you feeling, you know, with the …

GEORGE: Oh, not so great. But it is what it is.

CHARLIE: Yeah, shitty.

GEORGE: So sorry about you and Jenny splitting up. (*Pause a beat*) Was talking to your mother about it before.

CHARLIE: Yeah, right, anyway, these things happen. Jenny is coming to wish Mum a happy birthday anyway.

GEORGE: Oh that's nice. You know I don't think I've actually ever met her in person.

CHARLIE: Oh maybe not, we've hardly seen you over the years. You want to sit down, the chair next to Mum is for you. Want a beer?

GEORGE: I think I'll sit down Charlie. And I'll tell you what, a beer wouldn't go astray if you've got one.

CHARLIE: Sure, I'll get you one.

(George goes and sits next to BESSIE. He says something to her but she doesn't respond. They both sit looking straight ahead, GEORGE given his beer takes a sip.)

GEORGE: Ah, 5X. I really like this Aldi beer. Good. Different.

(Now that most of the players are on stage- the lighting will define where the conversation is – the whole stage, one group or another.)

GEORGE: This is nice isn't it? Having a picnic. Sitting next to my big sister. Catching up with Charlie and Martha.

BESSIE: *(No response)*

GEORGE: Charlie's doing well with the farm he tells me. Great life, and he comes to see you, what, a couple of times a week? That's great.

BESSIE: *(no verbal response, smiles vaguely)*

MARTHA: Look at them. Isn't that cute? Little brother and big sister like that?

CHARLIE: Yeah the perfect pair. She can barely talk …

ROSS: And he can barely hear.

MARTHA: Is Penny not back yet?

CHARLIE: Yeah, she's just in the van doing the salads.

MARTHA: I've had an idea.

CHARLIE: That's a worry. Never been a fan of your ideas.

MARTHA: Jenny's not here, so when Penny comes out you just tell her to pretend to be Jenny. Mum won't be able to tell the difference.

CHARLIE: There's a small flaw in that plan. What about when Jenny gets here?

MARTHA: Maybe she won't come after all, so we'll cross that bridge when we come to it. If we come to it. Penny's here so she has to be Jenny.

CHARLIE: I dunno. I'll try Martha. Not sure it's fair on Mum.

MARTHA: Just do it Charlie. It'll be fine. Mum doesn't have to know.

CHARLIE: I'll ask Penny, Martha. No guarantees though.

(*Lights down and spot on Bessie. She verbalizes her thoughts.*)

BESSIE: For a moment. A minute. Sometimes more. I can see clearly. That's a song isn't it? (*Sings*) "I can see clearly now the rain has gone". You see. I can remember some things, sometimes.

It's like I wake but time has passed. I don't know how long. I'm in bed looking at an empty ceiling. Or in a chair by a window. A window to a patchwork of trees and grass and flowers. A window to life. A window to a world I will never see properly again.

Then the cloud comes back. The fog. The rain gets in my eyes. Life, if this is life, is a blur. A blur of nothingness.

(Spot off and stage lights up. ROSS moves over next to GEORGE, taking a chair and sits next to him. Begins to talk to them both. Lights then focus on conversation between MARTHA and CHARLIE.)

MARTHA: She seems ok.

CHARLIE: Yeah.

MARTHA: Pretty much the same as when I saw her last time.

CHARLIE: On her 74th birthday.

MARTHA: Nooo?.... has it really been a year? I've been down since then surely?

CHARLIE: Nup.

MARTHA: Oh well. She probably hasn't noticed.

CHARLIE: Maybe not. *(Beat)* I've noticed.

MARTHA: What do you mean?

CHARLIE: I just know that you haven't been down since last birthday.

MARTHA: Well, it's not easy…

CHARLIE: And then the birthday before that. If only Mum had birthdays more often, she'd actually see you more often.

MARTHA: Charlie, I try. I'm doing my best. I've had a divorce.

CHARLIE: That's not exactly a full-time job. And from what I hear Colin was very generous in the settlement anyway. You didn't even have to go to Court.

MARTHA: Well, it still took its toll. On me. And the kids.

CHARLIE: Your "kids" are all fully grown adults. I think they can cope.

MARTHA: And we sold the house. I had to move.

CHARLIE: Yeah, into a commune. What's it called again? "Happy valley"?

MARTHA: It's not a commune. And it's not called "happy valley". It's called Harmony Hill.

CHARLIE: Oh, that's so much better.

MARTHA: (*Ignoring the snide comment*) It's a shared facility. On a farm. We just share most things we live on. It's very peaceful and harmonious. But it's not a hippy commune or anything. And I do work on the farm.

CHARLIE: Really?

MARTHA: I'm in charge of the beehives. We produce natural organic honey.

CHARLIE: Is there so much "harmony" that you have to share all that money from the divorce?

MARTHA: That's none of your business. Anyway, we don't have to share everything.

CHARLIE: Lucky for you.

MARTHA: And what did you mean "from what I hear Colin was very generous". Who did you "hear" from?

CHARLIE: Who do you reckon?

MARTHA: Colin. I'll kill him. My money has nothing to do with you.

CHARLIE: Apparently not.

MARTHA: What's that supposed to mean?

CHARLIE: Nothing

MARTHA: Charlie …. what are you saying?

CHARLIE: Nothing. (*Charlie has surrendered to Martha again*)

MARTHA: (*louder, getting cranky*) What exactly did Colin say to you?

BESSIE: (*calling out suddenly*) Colin! Where's Colin? Martha where's Colin?

MARTHA: (*Quietly to Charlie*) Oh shit.

GEORGE: Is Colin coming? I thought you two were divorced Martha.

MARTHA: (quietly) Oh double shit.

(George leaves Ross to go talk to Charlie. Lights and attention shifts to Martha and Bessie. It seems Bessie has retreated from the moment of apparent lucidity. Charlie is watching Martha talk to Bessie.)

MARTHA: So Mum, Colin and I are very happy.

CHARLIE: (*Aside*) That's because they're not married to each other anymore.

MARTHA: He just couldn't come today. He's very busy, and it's a long way. But Colin sends birthday hugs Mum. (*Pause a few beats*) Can you hear me Mum? Do you understand? Mum, everything's ok with Colin.

BESSIE: (*getting the words out with difficulty*)

Who's Colin?

MARTHA: Colin, you know Colin….

BESSIE: What's your name again dear?

(*Martha puts her hands in her head freezes as do the other characters. The spot comes on Bessie for another thought sharing moment, this time much more hesitant and shakier.*)

BESSIE: I don't understand. I try. I really try. These people. They think I'm supposed to know them. But I don't know them. When they talk to me I smile and nod sometimes. At least I think I do, I'm not sure what my face is doing. Maybe that's why I get funny looks. When I try to say something most of the time the words don't came out, they just stay in my head. With the other ones. They don't seem to get out much anymore. And then …

(*Pause and then Bessie goes into recall mode*)

Ernie, why is Charlie crying? Ernie? Ernie?

(*Penny enters from van carrying a couple of salads*)

PENNY: Hello everyone

(*Charlie rushes over and intercepts Penny. They have a conversation which the others cannot hear, but obviously know is happening.*)

CHARLIE: Penny, darling, (*leans forward and kisses Penny on the cheek*) thanks for the doing the salads. There's something … I need to call you Jenny.

PENNY: That's a bit weird Charlie.

CHARLIE: I mean just now, for the moment

PENNY: Still weird Charlie. We've been going out for 3 months, I think that's long enough for you to call me by my own name.

CHARLIE: Yeah but …

PENNY: (*Interrupting*) Just try it – "Pen- ny"

CHARLIE: (*Not trying, just wanting to talk to her*) Penny …

PENNY: (*Interrupts*) Good boy, well done.

CHARLIE: Penny..

PENNY: Twice in a row – great work.

CHARLIE: It's Martha's idea.

PENNY: No surprise there.

CHARLIE: I haven't told Mum that Jenny and I have split up. So Martha wants you to pretend to be Jenny, so Mum doesn't get upset.

PENNY: (*Slowly*) You haven't told your mother that you and Jenny split up after how many ever years it was???

CHARLIE: It sort of never came up. I didn't bother. And Martha ..

PENNY: You broke up 6 months ago and you haven't told her?

CHARLIE: Not 6 months, maybe 4, 5, and a half ....

PENNY: (*Sardonically*) Well there's a lovely birthday present for your Mum - tell her today Charlie. And that you have a new girlfriend who's much more gorgeous.

CHARLIE: No, please. Let's do what Martha asks. I don't have to tell Mum yet. Not today. Not on her birthday. Look, it doesn't really matter anyway ..

PENNY: Oh doesn't it?

CHARLIE: To her, I mean to her. She won't get it, she won't understand. Let's just keep Martha happy.

PENNY: Fuck Martha. Bloody hell. Jeeeeesus.

CHARLIE: Please. Please. Please. So there's no argument, please can you be Jenny just to wish Mum happy birthday and then you can go.

PENNY: Oh that's nice. Getting rid of me too.

CHARLIE: No, I mean, no, um, it's just that I thought you might want to, you know, go somewhere rather than put up with, this.

PENNY: Not particularly. I want to talk to your Mum.
           Keep in her good books.

CHARLIE: Ok, whatever…. But …. Jenny??

PENNY: Oh alright. But just for the party. Still really
           weird Charlie.

*(They both turn to face the others, everyone except Bessie is
looking at them. Charlie announces.)*

CHARLIE: Jenny's here.

(Charlie takes Penny to Bessie)

CHARLIE: Mum, Jenny wants to wish you happy birthday.

PENNY: Happy birthday Bessie.

BESSIE: Thank you dear. What did you say your name
           was?

PENNY: Pe.. (*quickly*) Jenny. I'm Jenny. Jenny. Jenny.
           Jenny. I'm with Charlie.

BESSIE: Of course you are dear, yes, yes.

(George has stood up)

CHARLIE: Uncle George this is Jenny.

GEORGE: Hello Jenny, nice to finally meet you.

PENNY: Definitely.

GEORGE: Very good of you to come….in the circumstances.

PENNY: (*Cautiously*) Circumstances, yes, well, wouldn't
           have missed it.

GEORGE: (*Trying to be* discreet) And I'm sorry about you and Charlie.

PENNY: Sorry? Oh, sorry …

GEORGE: Yeah, you two splitting up.

PENNY: Splitting up…

GEORGE: Charlie never mentioned any problems. Was a total surprise to me when he told me it was over.

PENNY: Me too, total shock, never saw it coming.

GEORGE: Really, that must have been hard.

PENNY: Oh yes, it was hard alright

(Penny decides to be a bit mischievous to get back at Charlie for making him pretend to be Jenny.)

            You'd never guess …

GEORGE: You don't have to explain.

PENNY: One day I came home after work, maybe a little early. Came to the van and went inside. And there he was.

GEORGE: There he was?

PENNY: With… another woman.

GEORGE: Oh dear.

PENNY: Yes, oh dear. But that's not all.

GEORGE   No?

PENNY: No. There was another woman.

GEORGE: Yes, you said that already.

PENNY: No. Another woman.

GEORGE: You mean …

PENNY: Yes, another woman and another woman. But there's more …

GEORGE: (*Interrupting*) Oh no more please.

(Meanwhile CHARLIE has been talking to Martha and Ross to bring Ross into the ruse with Penny/Jenny.)

ROSS: Dad, let ah Jenny talk to Bessie for a bit. Come and I'll get you another beer.

(George goes with Ross and Penny sits next to Bessie and Penny begins to mime chat to Bessie.)

END SCENE 6 (Lights dim for a few seconds)

SCENE 7

Today, a little later.

(Lights up and MARTHA is sitting next to BESSIE, MARTHA is miming a conversation with BESSIE. ROSS is talking to GEORGE.)

ROSS: They don't tell Bessie much of what is going on. Martha thinks it will upset her.

GEORGE: Well that's wrong. A parent is entitled to know the truth about their kids.

ROSS: Yeah, maybe, I agree, but it's not up to us. If they don't want to say then we shouldn't.

GEORGE: Bit late now.

ROSS: Not sure how much Bessie takes in.

GEORGE: Actually, I'm not sure how much Bessie takes in.

ROSS: Yeah, that's what I just said.

GEORGE: What?

ROSS: I said that's just what I said.

GEORGE: What did you say?

ROSS: I'm not sure how much Bessie takes in.

GEORGE: I'm not sure either.

(*Pause*)

ROSS: So, you keep in touch with Charlie?

GEORGE: Yes. I ring him. Or he rings me.

ROSS: Yeah? That's nice. What do you talk about?

GEORGE: I don't know. Just stuff.

ROSS: When did all this start?

GEORGE: What do you mean "all this"?

ROSS: The phone calls....

GEORGE: Oh I don't know. A while back. He's my nephew, I am allowed to ring him. Is that a problem?

ROSS: Of course not. But I'm your son.

GEORGE: I am aware of that.

ROSS: It's just that you don't ring me much.

GEORGE: I don't want to bother you.

ROSS: It's no bother.

GEORGE: You always seem so busy.

ROSS: Never too busy to talk to you Dad.

GEORGE: No?

ROSS: No

GEORGE: Remember the last time?

ROSS: (*Tentatively*) No, what?

GEORGE: The last time I called.

ROSS: Not particularly, why? You don't mean the fake heart attack do you? Not going to do that again I hope.

GEORGE: Well, I … oh, it doesn't matter.

ROSS: What doesn't matter Dad?

GEORGE: Don't worry about it. You're here now and that's great. Thanks for driving me up. (*Calls*) Charlie, how's this farm of yours doing? What are you actually growing?

END SCENE 7

SCENE 8

A little bit later. ROSS talking to GEORGE and BESSIE.

CHARLIE and MARTHA just sitting and looking into the distance.

ROSS: … So after that auction down the street I reckon our place is worth at least 2 mill more than what we paid for it only 18 months ago. Very happy.

(Phone rings, ROSS goes to pocket, pulls out phone and looks at it.)

Oh this is a work thing, I have to take it. Back in a minute.

(ROSS goes to edge of stage starting the conversation.) Hello ..

CHARLIE: *(Sort of to himself but MARTHA can hear)*

Wanker.

ROSS: (on phone a little away from the others)

Frank, hi …… another …. When do you …. right …. Right ….. yep, I understand. Sounds like a good one…. Just the short version …

(He continues to listen on the phone)

(Focus shifts to George and Bessie)

GEORGE: (*to BESSIE*) He does that a lot. Don't see him much but when I do that phone is never far away. Except he doesn't use it to call me. And I hardly bother calling him anymore. He never seems to have the time to talk.

You know the last time I called him? It was sort of "what can I do for you Dad?" and I said, "oh just catching up" and I could hear noise in the background. People. Talking, laughing. He just brushed me off. Asked if he could call the next day as he was tied up with "work stuff". "Sure" I said.

I wanted to tell him something, I really wanted to tell him something then and there, but it seemed he didn't want to talk to me. I knew he wasn't doing work or anything, he was just having friends over. And they were more important than talking to me.

(*GEORGE looks at Bessie for response. Nothing forthcoming. He goes on regardless.*)

I waited for his call back Bessie. All next day I waited. And waited. But he never called. And I never told him what I was going to tell him. At least he agreed to bring me up here. We sort of talked in the car. But more about nothing much. Football. Chit chat. I haven't been able to tell him yet.

You're lucky Bessie. You've got Charlie here who sees you all the time. And Martha too. She's here a lot she tells me.

BESSIE: (*Straining*) Martha.

GEORGE: Eh?

BESSIE: Martha.

GEORGE: What about Martha?

BESSIE: Martha comes. Who's Charlie?

(GEORGE looks to MARTHA as BESSIE "retreats" again.

GEORGE and BESSIE just sit in silence.)

(ROSS is on the edge of the stage but away from the picnic area. He is in the middle of his telephone call.)

ROSS: … I know it's important but it is Sunday…. But I'm out of Sydney and .. (*pause*) … of course … (*pause*) … look, best I can do is I'll look at it and call you when I get back to Sydney … (*pause*) I don't know, five or six hours … (*pause*) … three or four then… if I can get away …… it's a family birthday thing …. No, not really …. I'll get away as soon as I can … bye

(ROSS returns and sits next to GEORGE. Scene moves to MARTHA and CHARLIE.)

MARTHA: So what is it about my money Charlie? Are you jealous?

CHARLIE: Ha, no way.

MARTHA: Well what then?

CHARLIE: (*Reluctantly*) Well you could have helped a bit that's all.

MARTHA: Helped a bit? With what? Mum's in a nursing home and the pension covers everything as far as I know. And I see her when I can. And help with what anyway?

CHARLIE: You don't get it do you?

MARTHA: Get what? Charlie, stop talking riddles.

CHARLIE: Two ex-husbands, a bucketload of money, you buzz around with bees at bloody Harmony Hill and I'm stuck here. Looking after your mother.

MARTHA: She's your mother too. What do you mean stuck here?

CHARLIE: I mean stuck here. There's got to be someone, you know, like, not far away. That's what they said, you know that.

MARTHA: It was your choice Charlie. You chose to buy this "farm". That was your decision to live near Mum, no one forced you to.

CHARLIE: No? It was me or you and you said it couldn't be you. So you're saying I "chose" to be the one to look after Mum? I was the only one, Martha, the only one.

MARTHA: That's not true.

CHARLIE: And do you actually know how long it has been?

MARTHA: I dunno 4, 5 years.

CHARLIE: 7 years. 7 years. 7 years with no escape.

MARTHA: Charlie …

CHARLIE: And what do you do? Martha, how many times have you been here in that time? 7 times. Once a bloody year.

MARTHA: Charlie …

CHARLIE: And I go to the nursing home, two three times a week. I'm the one that's there. I'm the one that gets the phone calls if there's a problem. I'm the one who makes sure she has the drugs she needs. I'm the one. The only one. And you do nothing. Nothing.

MARTHA: Charlie, that's not fair.

CHARLIE: I'll tell you what's not fair. My whole life that's not fair.

MARTHA: Charlie, for heaven's sake, settle down. …. Don't do this now, it's Mum's birthday.

CHARLIE: Yes it is, and you know what? I can only let loose on her birthday because that's the only time you're here.

MARTHA: Charlie, I'm sorry you feel this way. I never thought there was an issue with you. Do you need money?

CHARLIE: It's a bit late now. You could have helped long before now. Come more, paid for the little things I have to find the money for. The extras, like chocolate or some medicine and stuff. It's not huge but I have to pay. You have never been here to really find out what's going on.

MARTHA: But she doesn't even know if I'm here or not. It's been that way for years.

CHARLIE: How do you know?

MARTHA: Well, it's obvious.

CHARLIE: Is it? Is it? Sometimes she sort of wakes up and actually makes sense. For a few seconds, or a few minutes. But you've never seen that. She could see you and hear you. If you were here. If you'd left your life of luxury more often you could have … told her that you love her, just talked to her. Or something. Just been here. We don't know what's going on in her head. No one does.

MARTHA: You've never asked me to come down more, or to give you money for things.

CHARLIE: I shouldn't have to ask. She's your mother too.

MARTHA: Don't blame me for you not telling me what's going on, or that you need money, or I should come more often. How should I know? It's your fault Charlie.

CHARLIE: It's always been my fault.

MARTHA: (*by now pretty upset*) Of course it is. Charlie, and look at yourself here

CHARLIE: What?

MARTHA: I mean I don't want to use the f word?

CHARLIE: What?

MARTHA: Failure Charlie. What are you actually doing with your life? Blaming Mum and me for you not getting out and actually doing something useful?

CHARLIE: I'm looking after our mother; I think that's reasonably useful.

MARTHA: Hardly a full time job Charlie. You just want to be the martyr. Charlie, the martyr. Dad always said you wouldn't come to much. And he's right.

CHARLIE: He made sure he was fucking right.

MARTHA: What is that supposed to mean?

CHARLIE: Don't pretend you don't know Martha.

MARTHA: I don't know what you're talking about Charlie.

CHARLIE: Oh yes you do. Don't pretend.

MARTHA: Charlie I reckon you're just here waiting for Mum to die? And wanting to get some money out of it.

CHARLIE: (*Quietly, CHARLIE has run out of fight again.*) Just forget it Martha.

(*This time everybody hears BESSIE.*)

BESSIE: Stop fighting you two. Martha, leave Charlie alone. (*Pause*) He may have started it but you don't have to keep it going. (*Pause*) Charlie, I don't know if it's your fault or not, just stop it. Charlie I said stop it. Oh now Martha's crying. And Charlie. (*calls out*) Ernie, Ernie can you sort these kids out, they're fighting again. (*Pause*) Stand up straight your father's coming. (*Pause*) I don't know what happened Ernie, I just heard the fighting and came out. (*Pause*) It's not always Charlie's fault Ernie. (*Pause*) (*A little anxiously*)

But go easy on him Ernie...... Ernie ... please .... not too much ... Martha go to your room ... don't make him cry Ernie ...

(Bessie retreats. Everyone is dumbfounded.)

ROSS: What was that all about?

MARTHA: I don't know. Some weird memory. I can't remember anything like that.

CHARLIE: (*Clearly shaken*) I can. (*To himself but audible.*)

MARTHA: Charlie?

CHARLIE: Nothing.

MARTHA: I thought you said something.

CHARLIE: No. It was nothing.

MARTHA: You said something Charlie.

CHARLIE: It was nothing Martha. Leave me alone.

ROSS: What about lunch? How about we get the table organised and get some food out here?

MARTHA: Good idea, come on up to the table Mum let's have some lunch.

(ROSS takes the opportunity to talk to GEORGE whilst the others bring food etc)

ROSS: Charlie has just told me that that's not Jenny, it's Penny.

GEORGE: It can't be, it's Jenny.

ROSS: I think Charlie would know.

GEORGE: But she told me about their break-up. Well, most of it. I didn't want to hear the rest.

ROSS: It's Penny pretending to be Jenny.

GEORGE: Not Jenny?

ROSS: No

GEORGE: Penny?

ROSS: Yep

GEORGE: Being Jenny?

ROSS: Yep.

GEORGE: Where's Jenny?

ROSS: Not here yet.

GEORGE: But that's Penny?

ROSS: Yep.

GEORGE: Who's Penny?

ROSS: The new Jenny apparently.

GEORGE: Is that why she's called Jenny now?

ROSS: No no no. It's just because Charlie hasn't told Bessie he broke up with Jenny. So Penny, his new girlfriend, is pretending to be Jenny. Ok?

GEORGE: That's just a little confusing …

JENNY: (*off stage*) Charlie!

CHARLIE: Oh shit, that's Jenny. Quick, um, Ross, can you show Jenny inside the van please?

ROSS: Jenny?

CHARLIE: That Jenny (*pointing to Penny*)

PENNY: I've seen inside the van … I do sort of live here most of the time.

CHARLIE: Have another look, please.

ROSS: "Jenny", let's look.

(*Ross and Penny go into the van.*)

(*Jenny enters, Charlie tries to intercept*)

CHARLIE: Jenny, hi, I just need you to …

JENNY: Charlie, you know I've never taken orders from you and I'm certainly not starting now.

(*Jenny goes over to Bessie*)

JENNY: Hi Bessie, happy birthday. (*Hands Bessie flowers*)

BESSIE: Thank you dear. They're lovely. What's your name again?

JENNY: It's Jenny.

BESSIE: Oh that rings a bell. Have you been here before?

MARTHA: She was here a little while ago and went away and came back. After changing her clothes.

JENNY: What? I just arr ….

(PENNY *enters from caravan with* ROSS *just behind.*)

PENNY: I'm not staying in here one minute longer. (*Sees* JENNY is here)

PENNY: What's she doing here?

JENNY: I was invited. What are you doing here?

PENNY: I live here.

CHARLIE: Well not really.

PENNY: Charlie!

JENNY: Charlie!

BESSIE: Charlie. I don't understand.

END SCENE 8

SCENE 9

Today, a little later

The picnic table is set. Bessie, Ross and George are seated. Penny and Jenny stand awkwardly at the side. Charlie is putting food on the table.

MARTHA: I'll cut up your meat in a sec Mum. Bet you don't get food this good at the nursing home.

CHARLIE: (*To himself*) I bet you don't actually know.

GEORGE: Jenny, Jenny, sit down why don't you?

PENNY: Oh Jenny was just going.

JENNY: No she wasn't.

PENNY: I'm pretty sure she was.

JENNY: I'm pretty sure she wasn't.

(JENNY *sits down at the table*)

PENNY: Well if she's staying, I'm staying. I didn't realise that ex's who dumped their boyfriends were invited.

JENNY: And I didn't know that certain people were allowed out without their parole officer supervising.

PENNY: And I didn't know that people who threaten
            to bring in the lawyers for something or other
            would have the hide to sit at the same table as…
            as….

JENNY: And I didn't know that money hungry devious
            slags who are only hanging around in the hope
            of screwing money out of a sad human being are
            not back in gaol.

CHARLIE: Oh for fuck's sake. What is going on?

MARTHA: Oh this is great. Charlie I told you Penny should
            have disappeared.

CHARLIE: Martha!

JENNY: I agree.

GEORGE: Why don't you both just stay? And we can sort
            all this out. Ross is a lawyer, maybe he can help.

ROSS: Dad, I'm not sure this is something I'd get
            involved in. Not really what I do.

GEORGE: Well I just thought you could have helped. Sit
            down both of you.

*(They sit down next to each other. Charlie serves them something
from the barbecue.)*

(Silence at the table)

CHARLIE: Mum, you remember Jenny (*Vaguely gesturing
            in their direction*)

BESSIE: Do I?

CHARLIE: And this is Penny. (*Vaguely gesturing in the same direction as before*)

PENNY: Actually, I'm Penny, Charlie's girlfriend.

BESSIE: But Charlie has a girlfriend. Called Jenny.

GEORGE: All his girlfriends are called Jenny it seems, Bessie.

JENNY: I'm Jenny, Bessie. I used to be Charlie's girlfriend, but we broke up.

GEORGE: And that's a story, I can tell you. Well, I can't tell you actually, it's a bit much.

PENNY: Bessie, I'm Charlie's girlfriend now.

BESSIE: I agree with George. I'll call you both Jenny whoever you are.

MARTHA: Charlie, you've ruined everything now.

CHARLIE: Shut up for once Martha, would you.

(*Awkward pause all round*)

ROSS: This is nice thanks Charlie.

CHARLIE: Good.

ROSS: Dad, you're not eating much. (*George ignores.*) (*Louder*) Dad, you're not eating much.

GEORGE: No need to shout.

ROSS: Well, I didn't think you heard me the first time. You didn't answer or acknowledge me.

GEORGE: I heard you; I just didn't acknowledge you.

ROSS: Is your food ok?

GEORGE: It's fine. Charlie has done a great job.

ROSS: Are you ok?

GEORGE: I'm fine.

ROSS: You sure?

GEORGE: I said I'm fine, didn't I? There's nothing for you
            to worry about.

ROSS: Fine.

CHARLIE: Uncle George, why don't you tell him? You really
            shouldn't leave it any longer.

ROSS: Tell me what? (*George ignores and pretends to
            eat.*) I said, "tell me what?". Is there some sort of
            big secret? Dad? Dad? Can you hear me? What
            is it?

GEORGE: I'm busy just now. I'll get back to you.

ROSS: Fine. (*To Charlie*) I reckon it's only me he doesn't
            hear.

GEORGE: I heard that.

MARTHA: Well cheers everyone, happy birthday Mum.

ALL: Happy birthday Bessie/Mum

BESSIE: Oh, is it someone's birthday? I do love birthdays.
            Charlie, do you remember your birthday last

year? Your first as a teen - 13 years old you were. We had such a lovely party. All the family came over.

(*Silence*)

CHARLIE: Yes, Mum I remember. Only, too, well. It was ...

JENNY: It's okay Charlie. You don't have to.

MARTHA: Charlie?

BESSIE: Your father was still alive.

CHARLIE: Yes, he was very much alive ... and kicking ...

JENNY: Charlie, maybe it's not the time.

MARTHA: Whatever it is, I'm sure it's not the time Charlie. Just eat your lunch

CHARLIE: That's it. I've had enough (*Shouting*)

MARTHA: Charlie?

CHARLIE: Martha, I'm tired of you telling me what to do. I'm tired of you telling me what to do for the last 30 years. I'm tired of wondering whether you would ever understand what I am going through, what I've been going through all my life.

MARTHA: Charlie, what the hell are you talking about?

CHARLIE: Yes Mum, Dad was alive alright. In his prime. (*Bitterly*) But it wasn't such a happy birthday for me. Martha, you should know that too.

MARTHA: I don't remember anything. Really Charlie, is this necessary? I think there's been enough surprises for today.

CHARLIE: It was what, 30 odd years ago; but I will never forget that day Mum. It wasn't a lovely birthday Mum. You know that.

MARTHA: Whatever it was Charlie, please don't say anything else. Let Mum have the happy memory. She obviously doesn't remember something bad happening.

JENNY: Not your call Martha.

ROSS: What are you talking about Charlie?

MARTHA: Leave it Charlie. Please.

CHARLIE: That's you all over isn't it Martha? Don't spoil a good story with the truth. Keep your head in the sand. Or in a beehive at happy valley might be better.

MARTHA: That's not fair Charlie.

CHARLIE: Isn't it? Isn't it?

MARTHA: I'm just trying to let Mum keep a happy memory.

CHARLIE: Life isn't always happy Martha. Haven't your divorces told you that? Or maybe not. Doesn't truth mean anything to you anymore? Mum should know the truth.

PENNY: It's that happy valley you live in I bet that's made you like this Martha.

MARTHA: You stay out of this!

CHARLIE: You didn't do anything then and you're not doing anything now. Not you. Not mum. No one.

MARTHA: About what Charlie? Am I supposed to know there was something going on?

CHARLIE: You knew.

MARTHA: What? What did I know?

CHARLIE: Don't pretend Martha.

MARTHA: I'm not pretending. I don't … oh my God …. Did he? Was he? (*Realization*)

CHARLIE: He was hitting me. Hard. Often. Only me. Never you.

ROSS: Hitting you? Uncle Ernie?

CHARLIE: Oh yes. He certainly did. I was his only son. Never living up to his expectations. His demand for, I don't know, perfection. At school, in sport, everything. And he hit me every time I failed in his eyes. And on my 13th birthday. I can't remember why anymore, just that I got a real walloping that day, after the party was over. Maybe I forgot to say thank you often enough. I have never been able to forget that beating.

MARTHA: Oh no. I never knew …. Well, I knew he punished you, but, oh Charlie …. I never thought …

CHARLIE: And you didn't do anything Martha, even though you were much older than me. You pretended it wasn't happening. You've always been wrapped up in yourself. Mum did nothing either. But maybe she was scared he might start on her. I don't know. It's no excuse though.

MARTHA: Oh, I'm so sorry Charlie. I don't know what to say.

PENNY: That's a pleasant change.

CHARLIE: And then when he died. I was, what, 15. I was happy. How bad is that? I was happy my father was dead. I was happy he'd gone from my life. There'd be no more beltings. I didn't have to walk around scared all the time.

And I thought that this, this, demand that I be perfect and succeed, would go to his grave with him. But it never did; it's stayed with me. I can't get it out of my head. That I have to meet this expectation of my father, my dead father. I never have. I never did. I never will.

And now too I feel so guilty that I wanted him dead, that I was so happy when he died. I'm so screwed up. An all-round class A screwed up, guilty fucking failure.

MARTHA: Oh Charlie, nooooo, you're not a ....

CHARLIE: Aren't I? Aren't I? Look at me now. Living in a caravan in the middle of nowhere, no money in the bank, chopping down trees that I hope no one notices, and have two girlfriends who pity me, apparently both called Jenny. One who understandably couldn't hang around with a loser anymore and one apparently who wants ...

I don't know what she fucking wants, but not me that's for sure.

MARTHA: Oh Charlie .... What can I say… ?

CHARLIE: Leave it Martha. Maybe just say nothing for once. I've had it with you. Just....just … stop.

PENNY: Jesus fucking Christ, you tell her Charlie.

CHARLIE: I need some air.

(*Charlie begins to walk off stage.*)

MARTHA: I'll come with you. We have to talk.

CHARLIE: No we don't Martha. I'll decide this time, not you. Maybe one day we'll talk Martha. Not now.

PENNY: I'll come with you baby.

CHARLIE: Why?

PENNY: Well …?

CHARLIE: Do you actually care about me?

PENNY: Of course I do Charlie baby.

JENNY: Bullshit, of course she doesn't. She just needs an address for her parole officer and hasn't got anywhere else to go.

PENNY: That is so not true. And who are you to talk Miss goody two shoes – you dumped him. Bitch.

CHARLIE: Oh, shut the fuck up, both of you. That's it. I don't want to hear any more.

PENNY: Charlie, baby, don't say that.

CHARLIE: I just said it, didn't I. No more. (*Pause*) Mum, if you're in there somewhere. I remember. I remember everything.

(*Charlie turns to leave*)

GEORGE: Charlie, let me come with you.

(*Charlie and George exit*)

(*Silence at the table*)

ROSS: Well, that was …. unexpected.

MARTHA: I had no idea, really, and he can be so dramatic. Is it really that bad?

JENNY: He always complained about you Martha. He never came to terms with what his father did, then Bessie got dementia, and you just left him Martha. Left him alone to do everything.

MARTHA: But you were there most of the time Jenny. Maybe if you'd stayed with him …. why did you two split up?

JENNY: Don't you dare think anything's my fault Martha. I did what I could. It just got too much. I tried to get him out of this sense of failure, but nothing worked. I couldn't go on in that situation, I couldn't live with Charlie like that all the time. He was taking me down with him.

MARTHA: (*To* PENNY) And then you came along ….

PENNY: Don't blame me for anything.

BESSIE: Charlie? Charlie?

MARTHA: He's gone for a walk with George, Mum. They'll be back soon.

BESSIE: Poor Charlie. I hope he's okay.

MARTHA: Of course he's okay, don't worry Mum.

BESSIE: I heard.

MARTHA: Heard what Mum?

BESSIE: I heard it all.

MARTHA: What do you mean Mum?

BESSIE: Tell Charlie I'm sorry. I knew. I always knew. But I couldn't, I couldn't, I wanted to, but Ernie wouldn't listen to me. He wasn't a bad man, Charlie, he wanted you to be like him, but you weren't. You were Charlie, not Ernie. But he never knew what to do, so he hit you. He was an army man Charlie, he went to war. But there was no excuse. Charlie, Charlie, Charlie, Charlie I'm sorry.

(*Bessie returns to silent reverie*)

(*George and Charlie return*)

MARTHA: Charlie ....

CHARLIE: Martha, enough already.

MARTHA: But Charlie, I need to tell you ...

CHARLIE: The only thing you need to do is apologise and maybe stay out of my life for a while.

MARTHA: Charlie, Mum heard everything you said.

CHARLIE: What?

MARTHA: She said she heard everything.

ROSS: That's true Charlie boy.

CHARLIE: Oh. (*Beat*) Well so be it, it's the truth. She must have known anyway. I just wish she'd stopped the beating. And you too Martha.

MARTHA: I couldn't Charlie. There was nothing I could do.

CHARLIE: You could have stopped being a self centred shit all your life.

MARTHA: Charlie! I'll let that slide at the moment. Mum, Mum, Charlie's back. Tell him what you told us.

(*No response from* BESSIE)

GEORGE: Bessie, Bessie. Do you want to talk to Charlie?

(*Still no response from* BESSIE *who even slumps a little more.*)

MARTHA: Mum said she is sorry Charlie. She tried and couldn't stop Dad.

CHARLIE: It's a bit late now isn't it? Not much point being sorry long after he's dead. She's just as responsible you know.

GEORGE: It's time to let it go Charlie.

CHARLIE: I want to hear it from her. I want her to tell me that she's sorry. That she knows what I've done for her, even though … (*he turns to* BESSIE) Mum, talk to me, talk to me.

GEORGE: Charlie. It's time. Let it go.

(CHARLIE goes to BESSIE and embraces her tearfully. BESSIE does not respond.)

CHARLIE: Oh Mum, I wish you ….

(ROSS'S mobile phone rings. ROSS looks at screen.)

ROSS: I have to take this.

(ROSS leaves table and moves to edge of stage.)

ROSS: Hello ….. no, still here …….soon …… I'm not sure, maybe an hour ….. ok, ok ….. I'll leave now ……. I'll call you back shortly.

(ROSS returns to the others)

GEORGE: Who was that?

ROSS: My New York client. I really have to go. Sorry.

GEORGE: The picnic's not over yet. I'm not ready to go.

ROSS: Sorry, but I really have to go. We've had an … interesting time.

GEORGE: I'm sorry but I don't want to go yet.

ROSS: Dad, you'll have to come with me. How else can you get home?

GEORGE: I don't know, I'll get a taxi.

ROSS: Really, a 200 kilometre taxi ride? Could you please say your goodbyes and we'll go.

GEORGE: No. I'm not ready to go yet.

JENNY: I'll take him home. George, I can take you whenever you're ready to go.

ROSS: Really? Would you?

JENNY: I'm going to Sydney anyway, to visit Mum.

ROSS: Well if you've got time to drop Dad home that'd be great.

JENNY: Can do.

ROSS: Problem solved. Dad, okay with you?

GEORGE: That's fine.

ROSS: We'll catch up soon.

GEORGE: Yep.

ROSS: Bye Bessie, happy birthday. Bye everyone. Thanks again Jenny.

(*Jenny waves acknowledgment to Ross*)

(*Ross goes to leave. Charlie gets up and follows. They talk at the side of the stage.*)

CHARLIE: Hey. You know you're a fuckwit.

ROSS: What?

CHARLIE: You're a fuckwit.

ROSS: Where's this coming from?

CHARLIE: Did your father make your life or any part of it a misery?

ROSS: No, of course not.

CHARLIE: That's why you're a fuckwit. Or at least partly. The rest of it is all your own work.

ROSS: Charlie, I don't know what the hell you are talking about.

CHARLIE: Someone's got to tell you. I've been wanting to all day. And now I am really in the mood. You're a fuckwit.

ROSS: What the hell Charlie?

CHARLIE: Why do you think George rings me? Why do you think he tells me stuff. Why do you think I talk to him?

ROSS: I don't know; maybe you've got nothing better to do.

CHARLIE: Because you don't have time for him. You don't talk to him. You hardly ever see him.

ROSS: Bullshit. I see him. I talk to him. You know he sent me a message saying he'd had a heart attack? I went over virtually straight away but it was nothing. That's what I have to put up with.

CHARLIE: Oh really? Have you actually thought about that? You've got no fucking idea.

ROSS: I'll call him this week. Definitely. I've got to go. (*Looks at watch*)

CHARLIE: He's a good guy, Ross. You should get to know him.

ROSS: I know him Charlie, he's my father. I'm going. (*Ross turns to go.*)

CHARLIE: Ross. Wait. You need to know.

ROSS: What?

CHARLIE: Your father is sick.

ROSS: What do you mean sick?

CHARLIE: I mean really sick.

GEORGE: (*Calls out*) You don't have to Charlie.

CHARLIE: (*Calls back*) He has to know Uncle George. (*Back to Ross*) Your father has got stage 4 bowel cancer. He may not have long left. Months, maybe weeks.

ROSS: Bowel cancer?

CHARLIE: Yep.

ROSS: How long has he known?

CHARLIE: A few months.

ROSS: How long have you known?

CHARLIE: A few months.

ROSS: Shit. (*Looks at watch*) Fuck.

CHARLIE: He wants to tell to you about it. He's been trying to for ages, but you don't give him the time.

ROSS: Shit. (*Looks at watch*) Fuck.

CHARLIE: You've got time now. Haven't you. (*Not a question.*)

ROSS: Shit. Fuck. (*Pause, looks at watch again*) I'll call him tomorrow. I've got to go. Call you tomorrow, Dad.

(*Ross exits. Charlie returns to table.*)

CHARLIE: I'm sorry Uncle George. I tried. He'll call you tomorrow.

GEORGE: You think?

CHARLIE: I think. I hope.

GEORGE: Me too. Thanks Charlie. That was a good thing you did. It was … brave.

CHARLIE: Nah, not really ….

GEORGE: And, thanks Jenny for giving me a lift. Much appreciated. I just … Bessie … last time … I … who knows … time … we've got … got left …

JENNY: Or any of us have got left.

PENNY: Fuck that's miserable, cheer up you lot.

CHARLIE: You got somewhere to go?

PENNY: Nah

CHARLIE: Not a question. You got somewhere to go.

MARTHA: Better late than never to disappear.

PENNY: Oh. I get the hint. I got somewhere to go. We'll talk later Charlie.

(PENNY *goes to* BESSIE *and embraces her*)

It's been so lovely meeting you Bessie. I hope to see you a lot more.

CHARLIE: Goodbye Penny.

PENNY: Bye everyone, it's been so much fun.

(*Penny exits*)

CHARLIE: Maybe time for the gifts?

MARTHA: There's no time like the present.

GEORGE: There's no present like time.

(*Ross enters and stands at the edge of the stage.*)

ROSS: Dad. I've got time.

END SCENE 9

SCENE 10

A chapel, represented simply by a few chairs and a lectern. CHARLIE and ROSS are standing by a lectern at the front. MARTHA enters and mimes greeting a few other people. JENNY comes in and waves to ROSS. MARTHA waves to CHARLIE and ROSS who respond.

ROSS then walks to the other end of the chapel and exits. Moments later ROSS enters pushing GEORGE in a wheelchair. GEORGE is wearing an oxygen mask attached to a bottle and a drip into his arm.

CHARLIE talks from the lectern.

CHARLIE: Good morning everyone. You all know I'm Charlie, Bessie's son. Before I hand over to the celebrant, I just want to say a few words.

First thank you to my sister Martha who has organised this celebration of Mum's life here at Happy Va.. sorry, Harmony Hill. She has done everything for today, including making the honey sandwiches, which I am sure we will enjoy later.

Second, a big thank you to my cousin Ross and his father George. My dear Uncle George is not very well at all, and Ross is now his full time carer. I know how hard it was for you to come all this way so it's great to see you both.

And thank you all for coming. I only met most of you today here at "The Hill" and I am grateful you have taken the time away from your yoga or meditation or hot Pilates or basket weaving to join us.

Finally, I don't want to cut across what Martha will say later, but can I just say that although Mum suffered from dementia for the last few years of her life, I think, I believe, that she knew more than she could say. There were plenty of moments of happiness for her I am sure, although it wasn't always possible to truly know.

In a way I put my life on hold to give her my time and to make sure she was cared for. I'm not sorry for that. She was my mother. I loved her with all her faults, and I guess with all my faults too.

Whatever was going on in that head of hers, none of us knew, but we believed, I believed, that there were moments when she knew, she knew everything that was happening and appreciated what people were doing for her. And the time I spent with her.

For me, it was a privilege to be her son.

CURTAIN

BUS STOP

SCENE

A bus stop comprised simply by a bench and a sign.

CAST

Edith, a widow aged 55-65

Mark, a single guy with a job aged 25-35

For most of the time Mark has white Apple earpods in his ears.
Will take them out when appropriate.

SCENE 1

The scene opens with Edith sitting at the bus stop. She sits straight and looks ahead somewhat blankly. There is the sound of a bus leaving.

MARK: (*from off stage, shouting*) Wait ……. Stop

Mark enters puffing.

MARK: Shit

Edith looks over to him. Mark does not notice Edith

MARK: Shit, shit, shit.

Edith: Language young man.

Mark: (*Not hearing or ignoring Edith*)

  Fuck it.

Edith: I said language young man

Mark: (*Noticing her*) Oh, sorry, but I just missed the fucking bus.

Edith: The what bus?

Mark: The f … , oh sorry. Sorry.. (*Beat*) (*To himself*) What am I going to do now?

Edith: There'll be another bus.

Mark: But that's not for, what, 25 minutes? I'll be late
                for work. On my first bloody day.

Edith   Dear me, that is a problem.

Mark: Did you miss the bus too?

Edith: No, I didn't miss the bus.

Mark: I'll have to get an Uber. (*looks at phone to book
                Uber*) That's going to cost me. Shit.

(*Mark keeps looking at phone*)

(*Edith gets up and begins to walk away.*)

Edith: Good-bye

Mark: (*Looks at Edith*) What? Oh… bye (puzzled)

                You're not catching a bus?

Edith: No

LIGHTS DIM

SCENE 2

Next morning (day 2)

Edith walks in and takes the same seat. Mark then runs in looking at his watch.

Mark: (*to himself*) Made it. (*Looks for the bus*)

Edith: On time today.

Mark: (*noticing Edith*) Oh hi. Yep. Won't miss it today. (*Still looks for bus.*)

Edith: Unless it came early.

Mark: (*Turns to Edith*) What? Did I miss it again?

Edith: No. It's never early. Well, almost never.

Mark: Ah, here it is. You getting the bus today?

Edith: No, not today.

Mark: For someone who doesn't catch the bus you seem to spend a lot of time at the bus stop (*laughs and gets on bus*).

Edith: (*To herself*). Yes. I do. I always have.

Edith watches bus depart and after a beat or two gets up, a hint of pain, and walks slowly away.

LIGHTS DIM

92

END SCENE 2

SCENE 3

Next morning (day 3)

Edith walks in and takes her seat. Mark walks in as soon as Edith sits.

Edith: Well, good morning.

Mark: Morning

Edith: Early today.

Mark: Yep. Getting into a morning rhythm now.

Edith: You're new to this area aren't you?

Mark: Yeah. Moved in last week. Renting a place a couple of blocks away.

Edith: Did you move to be near the bus stop?

Mark: (*Chuckles*) Not exactly. Moved down from the country and found this place not too far from my new job.

Edith: In the city.

Mark: In the city.

Edith: My husband worked in the city.

Mark: (*Uninterested, looking for the bus.*)

          Did he?

Edith: Every day for thirty odd years.

Mark: Aha.

Edith: (*Reminiscing, to herself really*)

          Every day

Mark: Aha (*Still barely listening, watching for the bus.*)

Edith: And every morning I'd walk with him to this very bus stop and see him go off to work.

Mark: (*Realising now what she is saying, turns to look at Edith*)

          What? Every morning?

Edith: Without fail.

Mark: He doesn't come with you to the bus stop now?

Edith: No.

Mark: Does he work from home?

Edith: Oh no.

Mark: Retired?

Edith: Not exactly.

Mark: What, he just can't work any more?

Edith: It would be a bit tricky.

(Sound of bus approaching. Mark gets up, start going towards bus.)

Mark: I'm sorry. I don't get it.

Edith: You're a bit slow aren't you? He's died.

Mark doesn't have the chance to say anything as the doors close and the bus leaves.

Edith stands up and gets a pain in her abdomen. Puts her hand on her stomach and bends slightly to relieve the pain.

Edith: Oooh. That hurts.

Edith quietly walks off.

LIGHTS DIM

END SCENE 3

SCENE 4

Next morning (day 4)

Mark enters looking at watch.

MARK: (*To himself*) Early this morning. I beat her.

Edith quietly walks to her spot on the bench, surprised to see Mark is already here. Before she sits Mark speaks.

MARK: Good morning.

EDITH: Good morning young man.

(Edith sits in her usual spot. Mark comes and sits beside her. Edith is more surprised and edges a little away from him. Mark tries to raise the subject about Edith's husband.)

MARK: So your husband doesn't work any more, I mean he doesn't catch the bus, I mean he doesn't really …. do anything … he's …

EDITH: I think you mean he's dead. That's right.

MARK: I'm sorry, that sucks.

EDITH: <u>You</u> might even say it's fucked.

MARK: Haha. Yep, it's definitely fucked. And I'm sorry, when you said it yesterday it didn't really sink in.

EDITH: It hasn't really sunk in for me either. Even after 6 weeks.

Edith grimaces in a little pain and holds her stomach.

MARK: You okay?

EDITH: Yeah, just a little indigestion or something.

MARK: So you come here without him though.

EDITH: Yes I can't get out of the habit. It's the way my day always started. Some quiet time, just the two of us. We'd walk here together, no TV, no radio and none of those white things you young people put in your ears.

MARK: You got kids though? Grandkids?

EDITH: No. We couldn't have children. Strangely that's what kept us close. Never found out why we couldn't. Whether there was something wrong with me or him. That didn't really matter. We didn't want to blame anyone. But we still had each other.

MARK: mmmm

EDITH: Until 6 weeks and 2 days ago. Now it's just me. Still walking to this bloody bus stop. I shouldn't say bloody really should I? This fucking bus stop. That feels better.

MARK: Is he with you?

EDITH: You do remember he's dead don't you?

MARK: I mean in spirit … while you walk here.

EDITH: Maybe he is, I don't know. But it'll feel like I've lost something more if I don't come here in the morning. It's like the pattern of my day, the routine, otherwise I'd just wonder whether I'd need to get out of bed at all. At least it's something to do.

(*Edith retreats into a reverie*)

(*Sound of bus approaching, Mark stands up, heads towards the bus.*)

MARK: Here's the bus. I'm Mark by the way. (*Beat*) (*Edith not focusing on Mark.*) You are .....

EDITH: (*still in reverie*)

Lonely.

(*Edith then shakes her head as if to wake up*).

Oh, I'm Edith.

Mark gets on the bus. After a few beats Edith leaves.

END SCENE 4

SCENE 5

Next morning (day 5)

Mark and Edith enter together, continuing to chat as they come on stage. Edith is noticeably more animated.

EDITH: Well that was quite lovely to have company. Thank you for joining me.

MARK: It's been a pleasure. I've enjoyed it too.

EDITH: Your family farm … it really takes me back. I loved being on our farm. I missed it so when my husband and I came to the city. He had to, you know, to get good work. And, well I didn't really have choice in those days. You went where your husband's job took him.

MARK: Yeah, I mean I liked it, but I was never going to be a farmer. My brother or sister will take it over one day.

EDITH: No one else wants to come to the city?

MARK: No, just me. The big move all by myself.

EDITH: Well I'm sure you won't be all by yourself for long.

MARK: Haha, well we'll see.

EDITH: I don't know how you found out where I live. Did you have a private eye on the lookout, or were you stalking me?

MARK: Ha, no. Well not really. I went for a wander about the neighbourhood last night and I just happened to see you putting out the bins. I didn't call out or anything, you might have thought that …

EDITH: … you were stalking me… (*jokingly*)

(*They both laugh*)

MARK: That's when I thought maybe we could walk here together.

EDITH: Well, I never. And you were on time too.

(*Sound of bus approaching*)

MARK: See you Monday Edith, at your gate?

EDITH: (*A little hesitation, then firmly.*)

            Yesss, I suppose so, yes.

Mark gets on the bus and Edith walks away with purpose.

END SCENE 5

SCENE 6

Two weeks later

Edith and Mark enter together talking.

EDITH: (*chuckles*) .... well, you'll have to talk to the landlord about those cockroaches.

They both sit

MARK: Um, yesterday, I waited a bit, but you didn't come to the gate for our walk. Everything ok?

EDITH: Of course it is. (*Hesitant*) Just had a sleep in. Ended up staying up late watching a repeat of *Vera*.

MARK: *Vera?*

EDITH: She's a marvellous detective in the north of England, you haven't seen it? Always catching the murderer.

MARK: No, seemed to have missed that one.

EDITH: You know I started watching and got half way through and realized I'd seen it before. But I couldn't remember who did it. So I had to watch it till the end.

MARK: Well I missed you.

EDITH: Oh come on Mark, why would you miss an old woman rattling on and on ..

MARK: When you put it like that …. But so far, I've not met anyone else in the neighbourhood. You're my only friend. If you don't mind me calling you a friend.

EDITH: Well, imagine that, I have a friend. (*Laughs, then clutches her abdomen*) ooh, I shouldn't laugh.

(*Sound of bus approaching. Mark gets up, a little concerned but doesn't mention the pain.*)

MARK: See you tomorrow, Monday I mean, friend.

EDITH: Good bye … friend.

LIGHTS DIM

END SCENE 6

SCENE 7

Monday

Same bus stop. There is an envelope on the bench.

Mark enters alone, a little flummoxed.

MARK: I wonder what happened. Maybe she slept in again. Is *Vera* on every night? I'll ask her tomorrow.

Mark then notices the envelope on the bench. He approaches with caution.

MARK: What's this? (*Holding the envelope, reads the addressee*)

       "For Mark."

(Mark sits – at the opposite end from the "Edith end". He opens the envelope and begins to read silently. The words of the letter are read off stage by Edith)

EDITH: "Dear Mark. I am sorry. I won't be there tomorrow."

MARK: I guess that means today. She must have written this yesterday.

EDITH: "It seems those little pains I've been having are somewhat more serious than I thought. I've been in hospital since Friday and I've been having some tests. I asked one of those young orderlies to take a letter to the bus stop early in the morning. I hope he did. Anyway the doctor said that – well they never really say what they mean do they – it's grim apparently."

MARK: (*Puts down the letter for a moment*) Oh no.

EDITH: "There's no more walking to the bus stop for me I'm afraid. It looks like there's not much walking anywhere."

MARK: Oh Edith, my poor friend.

EDITH: "I will miss my daily walk with you Mark. And I want to thank you for walking with me for the last few weeks. You have no idea how it made me feel. I didn't feel quite so lonely. I even looked forward to it each morning …"

MARK: (*Now getting pretty emotional*)

Edith, I never told you how much it helped me too. I'd found a friend.

EDITH: "Good-bye Mark. I am sure you will make new friends in time. You have time Mark, that's the privilege of the young. Thank you. Much love. Your friend, Edith"

MARK: Shit, here's the bus.

Sound of bus in the distance, Mark stands and he pulls out a handkerchief to wipe his eyes. Sound of bus pulling up. Mark waves it on. The bus leaves.

Mark then goes to the spot where Edith used to sit and sits down in contemplation. In the same manner in which Edith used to sit.

From off stage a female voice calls out.

FEMALE: Stop…. Wait ….. Shit …..

Mark looks to the direction of the voice.

BLACKOUT/CURTAIN

MANHOOD

SCENE

A nondescript corridor with a door at the end, preferably at right angles to the corridor. There are two chairs side by side in the corridor.

CAST

Roslyn, stage age 35-45, old enough to be a parent of a 16 year old. Married to Peter.

Peter, stage age 35-45, old enough to be a parent of a 16 year old. Married to Roslyn.

The play opens with Ros apparently talking to someone through the doorway.

ROS: No, I understand. He shouldn't be too long. Thanks.

Ros is handed a mobile phone from the doorway,

ROS: Right, thanks.

Ros sits and examines the phone for half a minute or so.

Peter enters, a little urgently without really rushing. He bends and pecks Ros on the cheek.

PETER: Hi darl.

ROS: Hi.

PETER: What's happening?

ROS: You're late. Again.

PETER: Sorry. You know. (*beat*) Work stuff.

ROS: This is important.

PETER: So's work stuff. Anyway, should we go in?

ROS: When you weren't here on time, the Principal said he'll do a short Zoom meeting and he'll be ready in about another 10 minutes.

PETER: So I'm early after all. Good on me. (*Cheerfully*)

ROS: Yeah, good on you.

PETER: Is Andrew supposed to be here?

ROS: No, he wants to talk to us alone.

Peter sits in the vacant chair.

PETER: What's this about anyway?

ROS: You didn't read the email?

PETER: What email?

ROS: From the Principal.

PETER: (*Hesitating*) Ah, that email. Just a quick look.

ROS: You didn't read it did you? Really Peter.

PETER: I saw what time we had to be here…

ROS: I rang you and told you what time to be here. And you were still late.

PETER: So what's it all about?

ROS: Here. I didn't think you'd read it so I printed the email. Read it. And weep.

Ros hands over copy of email. Peter reads to himself then, puzzled says out loud…

PETER: "…. used a carriage service …" what's a carriage service? Has he been on a horse and cart? (*Laughs*)

ROS: It's the fancy word for a phone.

PETER: Oh. (*Reads again*) "…. used a carriage service to transmit unsolicited material which may offend…" What's that supposed to mean?

ROS: He sent a dick pic.

PETER: A dick pic?

ROS: A dick pic.

PETER: A dick pic?

ROS: A picture of his dick.

PETER: I know what a dick pic is. But he's what 14? There's nothing to see. Did he use a telephoto lens? (*Chuckling*)

ROS: He's 16 and no, he didn't.

PETER: Ok 16, but still, only 16…. what could he show?

ROS: The Principal gave me his phone.

Ros gets the image up on the phone.

Look for yourself

Peter looks at phone. Then takes phone from Ros. Takes a little time to look.

PETER: Oh. (beat) Ohhhh…… (beat) ooohhhhh…. Weeellll

ROS: Yes.

PETER: I mean he's ….

ROS: Yes.

PETER: Good photo, nice angle.

ROS: Peter!

PETER: (*Chuckles*) At least it's not an action shot.

ROS: Peter, come one, this is serious. He should not have sent that photo.

PETER: (*with little sincerity*) Of course, you're right. This is serious.

(*Peter hands back phone*)

PETER: Who did he send it to?

ROS: A girl at St Catherine's.

PETER: Girlfriend?

ROS: No.

PETER: There was no request for the photo?

ROS: Definitely not.

PETER: A cold call dick pic eh? That's brave. Did she reply?

ROS: Yes she did.

PETER: In kind? (*Smiling*)

ROS: Well, no photo, just some dirty language.

PETER: (*Keenly*) Ooo, show me.

            (*Ros hands Peter the phone*)

            Peter reads out loud from the phone

            "Fuck off. You're dead meat."

            Right. Not quite in the spirit he hoped I guess. You know, his meat certainly doesn't appear to be dead in that photo.

ROS: For fuck's sake Peter (*angrily but whispering so as not to be overheard*). I don't know why he'd do this. Something to do with the boys he hangs around with I'll bet.

PETER: Well boys will be boys.

ROS: What's that even supposed to mean? Some sort of excuse?

PETER: No, no, …… of course not.

Awkward silence

ROS: Have you ever sent a dick pic?

PETER: Never sent one to you.

ROS: No, I have to put up with the real thing.

PETER: Not very often.

ROS: What's that supposed to mean?

PETER: Nothing, nothing.

ROS: It's not as though you're knocking down the door to get into my pants.

PETER: Well when there's clearly no invitation ....

ROS: What, you need a written invitation now? "Dear Peter, please come home and fuck me instead of staying late at work or wherever you are. So long as you are sober." I'll remember that in the future.

PETER: Come on Ros, don't be like that.

ROS: Have you ever sent a dick pic?

PETER: Why would I do that?

ROS: Maybe it's something you do for fun with "the boys". You seem to find this situation somewhat amusing.

PETER: No, this is not amusing. Surprising... but not amusing. Definitely not amusing.

ROS: You still haven't answered my question.

PETER: Oh come on Ros, love. Let's stay on track. I mean next thing you'll be asking me if I'm having an affair.

PAUSE (at least 10 seconds)

ROS: Are you having an affair?

PETER: Now why would you say that?

ROS: You suggested it.

PETER: No I did not.

ROS: Well?

PETER: Come on, what are we doing about our boy, ...
            young man, ... man-boy and this .... dick pic?
            What'll it be? A rap over the knuckles?

ROS: More than that. He could be expelled.

PETER: Oh surely not. Not just for a dick pic.

ROS: Maybe he should be expelled. So he learns his
            lesson.

PETER: No way. He's just a boy. It's a boy thing. Part of
            growing up. Expressing his manhood.

ROS: That photo was no boy thing. You do realise it's
            sexual harassment don't you? She didn't ask to
            be sent ... that ...

PETER: But it's just a dick pic!!

ROS: It is never just a dick pic. When will you understand
            that? The girl is probably traumatised.

PETER: She'll get over it. Getting expelled will destroy
            Andrew.

ROS: You really think so? Have you ever spoken to
            him about this place? Do you actually know
            whether he likes it here, this old private school
            of yours? When was the last time you talked to
            him, I mean really talked to him. Or do you just
            talk dick pics to him? What a great example.

PETER: (*Looking around*) Come one, not now. Let's get this over with and we'll talk tonight.

ROS: Something else we don't do very often.

PETER: Well maybe tonight's the night – we can tick both the boxes. (*Chuckles*)

ROS: So you won't be late then.....with all the "box ticking" to be done.

PETER: Not really late, but there's a work thing I have to go to.

ROS: Another one. Will you be sober when you get home this time?

PETER: Of course I'll be sober, especially if we're ticking boxes...

AWKWARD SILENCE

ROS: Who have you sent dick pics to?

PETER: What are you talking about? Do we have to do this now?

ROS: Yes we do. Who? Show me your phone.

PETER: Come on Ros, don't you trust me?

ROS: Actually, I'm not sure that I do right now.

PETER: Fine, I confess. Maybe once, or twice. At the office as a joke.

ROS: I can understand that a picture of your penis would be a joke.

PETER: (*Peter stands*)

(*To himself*) Not everyone thinks that.

ROS: What?

PETER: Nothing. Why are we arguing? We're here about Andrew.

ROS: And you're not taking it seriously.

PETER: I am. I certainly don't want him expelled. That would be the worst.

ROS: I'm not so sure.

PETER: Come on, how would it look do you think? This is my old school. I'm on the old boys' committee. People know me. If my only son was expelled …

ROS: This is all about you isn't it? That's all you care about. Not that St Catherine's girl. Not Andrew. Not… me. That's you all over. I should have realized it long ago. It's always just about you. I don't know why I …

PETER: (*Interrupting*) Come on, come on, of course I care about you, and Andrew. And this girl. It's just, well …. I don't know…

(*Peter's phone buzzes with a message. He looks at the phone.*)

PETER: When is this happening? I'll really have to go soon.

ROS: Alright go now.

PETER: What?

ROS: Just. Go.

PETER: If... that's ... okay .... (*puzzled*)

ROS: Yes, you can go. I will deal with this.

PETER: Well you know what I think. It should be a rap
                on the knuckles, no more.

ROS: I know that's what you think. And I know what
                I think. About everything.

PETER: Right see you later tonight.

ROS: Ring before you come home please.

PETER: Sure, but there's no need to get any food for me,
                I probably will have already eaten.

ROS: Just ring. There's something I want to do before
                you get home.

PETER: What write an invitation?

ROS: Not exactly. Not tonight. (*to herself*) Quite the
                opposite I think.

PETER: Right, ok. See you later.

*Peter leans in to kiss Ros but she turns away. Peter exits. The
Principal's door opens.*

ROS: (*To Principal*) Yes, I'm ready. It's just me, Peter
                had to go. Anyway, I think we've just separated.

CURTAIN

FANTASY

CAST

Clare   Married/partner to Ryan
Ryan   Married/partner to Clare
Jan   Married/partner to Mike
Mike   Married/partner to Jan

All aged 30s or early 40s

SCENE

A home dining table. The characters, friends, are well into a dinner party. Not intoxicated but jolly enough.

The scene opens with general laughter, in response to a story told by Mike.

MIKE: It was so ridiculous.

JAN: I don't know how many times I've heard that, and it gets further and further from the truth every time. I'll take the dishes.

RYAN: (*Standing*) Let me help.

JAN: No, that's fine, you're our guest. My husband should do the helping. Mike? Mike?

MIKE: (*Distracted*) Oh, what? Sorry, of course. (Mike begins to stand)

RYAN: Sit down mate, I've got this. And Jan, I do object to being called a "guest" in my best friends' house – this is practically a second home to Clare and me we're here so often.

JAN: Just shut up and bring the dishes.

(Ryan and Jan exit)

(Pause while Mike and Clare wait for the others to leave dining room)

(The conversation between Clare and Mike is in whispered tones)

CLARE: I think it's time.

MIKE: No.

CLARE: Why not?

MIKE: Just … not yet.

CLARE: Then when?

MIKE: Soon.

CLARE: Tonight is soon.

MIKE: Too so…

(*Mike stops mid word as Jan and Ryan re-enter*)

JAN: Oooo, I hear whispering, what are you two plotting?

RYAN: I hope it's a surprise 40th for me next month.

MIKE: Well if I told you mate, it wouldn't be a surprise, would it?

RYAN: Good. Enough said, just let me know the date.

MIKE: Ha ha, very funny Ryan (*ironically*)

(*Ryan and Jan by now are seated. Pause in conversation while everyone relaxes, has a drink, sits back in their chair etc*)

RYAN: I know, let's play a game.

JAN: Good idea. What about "truth or dare"? Love that game.

RYAN: Yeah.

MIKE: Nah, not a fan.

CLARE: Why not? It's good fun.

MIKE: It's just …. it can get a bit personal sometimes. You know, sometimes the truth is tricky. (*Looks at Clare, silently pleading.*)

JAN: My dear husband, (*American accent*) You can't handle the truth. (*Teasing*) Oooh, darling what secrets are you hiding from me after 6 years of marriage?

MIKE: (*Forced chuckling*) Nothing … but I wouldn't want my secret life as a porn star to come out.

(*General laughter*)

RYAN: God, imagine you a porn star, that is hilarious.

JAN: What would be your porn name do you think?

CLARE: I know, Seinfeld, use George Costanza's porn name – Buck Naked. Love to see that.

(*General laughter*)

RYAN: I know, speaking of buck naked, here's a question. Who is your hall pass?

CLARE: Hall pass?

JAN: If you could sleep with someone else, anyone in the world, just the once, who would it be?

RYAN: So many options.

MIKE: That's easy. Emma Stone.

JAN: Yeah Mike, she'd just jump at the chance too.

MIKE: That's not the point, we're fantasizing. But she might like Buck Naked!

JAN: I think I'd go for Daniel Radcliffe…. Such a hunk now but dressed as Harry Potter.

MIKE: Yes, the schoolboy fantasy, going for the pretend young one.

JAN: Well, it makes a nice change.

RYAN: I'm thinking a little more mature.

MIKE: Not a school boy?

JAN: That's not what I meant.

RYAN: Ha ha, let's keep it legal. Emma Watson.

MIKE: Good choice. Dressed as Hermione Grainger?

RYAN: Not strictly necessary. But could be interesting. She probably needs to be a bit more slutty than Hermione Grainger.

JAN: Righto Clare your turn. Who is your fantasy?

CLARE: Oh, I don't know, let's move on.

RYAN: Come on, play the game. Who'd you pick?

MIKE: There must be some (*emphasizes*) movie star or someone else famous you'd fancy.

JAN: Do you really have to think that hard?

CLARE: (*Pause*) Alright … Michael.

JAN: Michael. Which Michael? Michael … Caine? Surely not. Too old.

CLARE: Nooooo

RYAN: Michael Jordan

JAN: Too tall.

CLARE: No.

MIKE: Michael J Fox?

RYAN: Nah, too shaky.

JAN: Ryan, that's awful, you can't say that. We give up Clare, which Michael?

CLARE: (*Nods to the other end of the table*) Michael.

RYAN: (*Pointing*) Him?

JAN: This Michael? Mike? My husband Mike?

CLARE: Yes.

(*The table goes silent*)

JAN: Well that's a surprise.

RYAN: Does he have to be in school uniform?

CLARE: Oh Ryan, ha ha. I was just answering your silly question.

JAN: So how long have you been fantasizing about sleeping with my husband?

CLARE: It's nothing Jan.

RYAN: So he's your fantasy fuck. How do you feel about
            it Mike? You up for it?

MIKE: Well it's flattering I'm sure. And a bit weird
            though. I mean it's not going to happen, it's
            hypothetical.

RYAN: Well here's a hypothetical question. Let's say I'm
            okay with it. Will you fulfill what is apparently
            my wife's fantasy?

MIKE: That's ridiculous.

JAN: Is it? I'd like to know the answer.

CLARE: Come on, it was just a game. Why are you all
            taking it so seriously?

RYAN: Because the prospects of me screwing Emma
            Stone are laughable and non-existent. That's the
            idea. You pick someone unattainable – a fantasy
            that can never be fulfilled.

CLARE: And you think Mike is not unattainable? Or is
            attainable?

RYAN: He's a lot more attainable than Emma Stone.

JAN: Or Harry Potter.

RYAN: Or Emma Watson.

MIKE: I'm not "attainable". Why would you think I'm
            so attainable.

JAN: Because you've got a dick. Dicks speak louder
            than words.

MIKE: Come on, my dick and I are very close but I wouldn't let him call the shots. I wouldn't be unfaithful to you Jan.

JAN: If I said it was okay to do it, just once, that means you wouldn't be unfaithful to me. You'd be free as a bird.

MIKE: So you're asking me, would I have sex with Clare just the once to fulfill her fantasy if you and Ryan are okay with it.

JAN: Yes.

MIKE: No

JAN: Why not? Because you're scared the reality wouldn't live up to the fantasy?

MIKE: No, I'm sure it would. You know, Buck Naked and all that.

JAN: Oh really, that's confidence.

MIKE: I don't know why you're getting cranky at me. It's not my fantasy.

JAN: Are you sure? You seem to be enjoying this.

MIKE: Not any more I'm not.

JAN: So Clare, what is it about Mike that makes him your fantasy choice.

RYAN: It's obviously not his intellect.

MIKE: Hey …

RYAN: Or his looks.

JAN: He is sort of funny looking.

MIKE: Thank you very much.

CLARE: Why is Daniel Radcliffe, or is it Harry Potter, your fantasy?

JAN: Because Daniel Radcliffe is a movie star, he's gorgeous, talented, probably straight, and I'll never meet him in my life, let alone look down and find him pumping away between my legs. He's a true fantasy.

RYAN: How long has this been going on?

CLARE: Nothing's "going on" Ryan.

JAN: Except in your dreams.

CLARE: It's just a fantasy Jan.

JAN: For now. What were you two talking about when Ryan and I were in the kitchen?

CLARE: I don't remember. Nothing.

JAN: You never said how long you've had this fantasy Clare. How long have you been dreaming of hopping into bed with my husband?

CLARE: Okay, okay. Since …. high school.

JAN: High school!!??

RYAN: You two weren't even at the same high school.

MIKE: No, I went to a boys school.

RYAN: With me. I didn't even know Clare then. How did you two know each other?

CLARE: We just met. At the beach during summer.

JAN: How old were you?

CLARE: Old enough.

RYAN: Old enough for what?

CLARE: Just… old enough.

RYAN: (*to Mike*) I remember now, you boasted about a summer fling, that you hooked up with someone. You never told me who it was. You said I didn't know her.

MIKE: You didn't.

RYAN: Until I married her eh? You bastard, you never told me you'd screwed my wife.

MIKE: Come on Ryan, everyone has had other partners before they got married, it wasn't relevant.

RYAN: Maybe not to you, but it would have been nice for me to know. You were my best man for heaven's sake.

JAN: Was that the only time?

MIKE: Yes.

RYAN: Are you sure? Clare?

CLARE: I'm sure. I didn't see Mike after that summer until you started going out with him years later Jan. And you two got serious very quickly.

JAN: And you never said a thing.

CLARE: How could I? I felt so awkward, and it got worse as time went by.

JAN: You felt awkward …?

CLARE: What good would it have done to tell you anyway Jan? You'd have hated me.

JAN: At least I'd have known. Instead of finding out now. I could have hated you for so much longer.

RYAN: That must have been tricky. After, what 10 years, your teenage crush in the arms, and bed, of someone else??

CLARE: I thought by then my life would be with you Ryan. I really did.

RYAN: Did you mean what you said in our vows?

CLARE: Yes Ryan, I do love you…

RYAN: But. (Pause) I can hear a "but" coming.

CLARE: But ..

JAN: What Clare? But what? After all these years you want to fulfill your fantasy. See if it feels the same as shagging on the sand when you were, what, 16?

CLARE: No that's not it. Mike and I …

MIKE: We want to get together. Not just once, but …

CLARE: For good.

RYAN: That's a hell of a "but". Clare you want to leave me. To live with my best friend. What if Buck Naked here is a lousy fuck after all? Are you going to be knocking on my door begging to come back?

CLARE: No, it won't happen that way. I know what I'm doing Ryan. You don't think Mike and I haven't talked about this? I won't be coming back.

JAN: What's going on Mike? I don't understand. Have you and Clare been having an affair all this time?

MIKE: No we haven't. We respect you and Ryan too much.

JAN: Jesus, you're dumping me for one of my best friends, that's really respectful.

MIKE: I'm sorry Jan, I want to be with Clare. I can't go on living a lie.

JAN: A lie! Our whole marriage has been a lie? My life is based on a lie? You never loved me did you Mike? Is that what you're saying?

MIKE: No, look, I don't know Jan. My head is all over the place. All I know now is that Clare was my first love and I think I never really stopped loving her. It was the biggest mistake of my life not to go and find her. And my second biggest mistake was …

JAN: (*Interrupts*) … marrying me.

MIKE: No, not that. It was not to tell you about Clare when we first started getting serious. And now I've hurt you more than I ever … ever…. I never wanted to hurt you. But I can't stop thinking about Clare, and being with her.

CLARE: I'm sorry Jan, I'm really sorry Ryan. I thought we'd be okay, I really did. But seeing Mike again when you introduced me to your mates, stirred something in me so much. But he was going out with Jan and I couldn't ask Mike to break up with her. And we see each other so often these days ….

RYAN: So what happens now?

MIKE: We thought we could get your blessing.

JAN: "Go to hell." Is that a blessing?

RYAN: Or maybe "get fucked" is a blessing?

MIKE: Please. We'd sort of hoped you'd understand.

RYAN: Really? It's a bit much to expect us to get this dumped on us, and then say "oh fine go ahead and ruin our marriages which are based on lies anyway".

JAN: I think you should go Mike.

MIKE: Yeah, I'll go to a hotel or something. (*To Jan*) I'll ring you tomorrow.

JAN: Gee, won't that be nice. I look forward to it. Will you have any earth-shattering announcements you've left till tomorrow? You're moving to Las Vegas so your alter ego "Buck Naked" can pursue his porn career? (*Turning to Clare*) Or you're pregnant? God you're not pregnant, are you?

CLARE: No Jan. Mike. I'll come with you now.

MIKE: Are you sure?

CLARE: Absolutely. I'll just grab my bag.

(*Clare exits*)

JAN: I need to go to the bathroom. I might just throw up.

(*Jan exits*)

(*Ryan and Mike stand uncomfortably*)

RYAN: That's it then.

MIKE: I guess so.

RYAN: Here's Clare, you'd better go.

(*Clare enters*)

CLARE: Good-bye Ryan. I'm sorry. (*Moves in to kiss him on the cheek. Ryan pulls back.*)

RYAN: No, just go.

(*Mike and Clare leave*)

RYAN: (*Big sigh as Jan returns*). Well, that's over.

JAN: They've gone?

RYAN: Yep.

JAN: Didn't wait to say goodbye to me.

RYAN: It was pretty uncomfortable; I think they just wanted to get out of here. It won't last, you know, that relationship, if you can call it that. They're dreaming, fantasies don't come true.

JAN: And there's no coming back. I hope they're feeling guilty.

RYAN: They were definitely feeling guilty.

JAN: As we intended they would.

RYAN: As it was meant to be.

JAN: I'm still amazed you found out about them.

RYAN: He's not exactly a good drinker that soon to be ex-husband of yours. It was a bit careless to let it slip out down at the pub, without even realizing, after he'd had a few. It was pretty clear to me he was besotted with her. And she still wanted him. Which frankly, was pretty convenient.

JAN: For us.

(*Jan and Ryan approach each other.*)

It was a beautiful plan. It bloody well worked a treat.

RYAN: It couldn't have gone any better. Hey, your Daniel Radcliffe line was a cracker.

JAN: Thank you, I was proud of it. Been practising for weeks… and your line about his intellect was hilarious.

RYAN: And true.

(*They both laugh.*)

(*They begin to embrace*)

RYAN: They're out of our lives.

JAN: At last.

(*Jan and Ryan kiss passionately*)

CURTAIN

www.ingramcontent.com/pod-product-compliance
Lightning Source LLC
Chambersburg PA
CBHW040537170726
48295CB00012B/501